Nocturnal Symphony

A Bat Detector's Journal

Book design by Jake Slavik
Illustrations by Arpad Olbey (Beehive Illustration)

Design Elements: Shutterstock Images

Published in the United States by Jolly Fish Press, an imprint of North Star Editions, Inc.

First Edition
First Printing, 2019

Library of Congress Cataloging-in-Publication Data
Names: Watson, J. A., 1980- author. | Olbey, Arpad, illustrator.
Title: Nocturnal symphony : a bat detector's journal / by J. A. Watson ; illustrations by Arpad Olbey.
Description: First edition. | Mendota Heights, MN : Jolly Fish Press, an imprint of North Star Editions, Inc., 2020. | Series: Science Squad | Summary: "Bru has two major goals to accomplish this summer: to help her Science Squad raise money for bat detection equipment, and to convince her mom to marry her longtime girlfriend"— Provided by publisher.
Identifiers: LCCN 2018050131 (print) | LCCN 2018053909 (ebook) | ISBN 9781631633010 (e-book) | ISBN 9781631633003 (pbk.) | ISBN 9781631632990 (hardcover)
Subjects: | CYAC: Bats—Fiction. | Mothers and daughters—Fiction. | Science projects—Fiction. | Moneymaking projects—Fiction. | Lesbian mothers—Fiction. | Gay parents—Fiction. | LCGFT: Fiction.
Classification: LCC PZ7.1.W4155 (ebook) | LCC PZ7.1.W4155 No 2019 (print) | DDC [Fic]—dc23
LC record available at https://lccn.loc.gov/2018050131

Jolly Fish Press
North Star Editions, Inc.
2297 Waters Drive
Mendota Heights, MN 55120
www.jollyfishpress.com

Nocturnal Symphony

A Bat Detector's Journal

by J. A. Watson

Illustrations by Arpad Olbey (Beehive Illustration)

Text by Anne E. Johnson

Consultant: Dr. Christopher Yahnke,
Professor of Biology, University of Wisconsin—Stevens Point

Fundraising Flop No. 1

To future historians who find this journal, here's some advice:

1. Long streams of paper towel taped together and tied to your friend's back with string make decent moth wings. Until it rains. Then they just turn into drippy white glop.

2. Always get permission from the librarian before you act out a dramatic skit inside the library. Apparently "But it's raining outside!" is not a good enough excuse. Neither is "But it's to raise money for Science Squad."

I blame Laura. The skit was her idea. She'd read something online about this library in a palace in Portugal that lets bats live in its walls. At night they fly around the stacks, eating the moths so the moths don't eat the library books.

Laura sounded so reasonable when she described her theatrical vision: "TK can be a moth. You'll be a bat. I'll be the narrator. And the director. Plus, I'll pass around a bucket for donations."

"Shouldn't we do a skit about Wisconsin bats?" TK dared to ask. "After all, we're trying to raise money to detect the sound of bats in Wisconsin. Not some palace in Portugal."

That question got the expected response: Laura's eyebrows formed an upside-down V, and her mouth made a sound like a whinnying horse. "TaKwon Davis, can you find a better bat-in-the-library story?"

TK shook his head and shot me a terrified glance.

"That's what I thought. You can tape paper towels together to make moth wings. And, Bru, you can use a black or brown blanket for bat wings."

So, it was settled—at least Laura seemed to think so. And, of course, it was a disaster.

I couldn't find any black or brown blanket or any kind of dark-colored cloth, so my bat wings were made of blue-and-white-striped sheets. Mom let me cut them up because they were worn out. In our basement I found a headband with little brown plastic ears, so I wore those, but they made me look more like a chihuahua than a bat.

We started the "play" with me chasing the moth (aka TK) around the bushes in front of the Ingotville Public Library. Laura gave a speech to the few snickering people who bothered to stop. Honestly, with all the running and flapping, I didn't hear everything she said. It involved key phrases like "bats are insectivores" and "beneficial to our ecology," and most importantly "Please give money to Science Squad." She held out the little blue plastic beach bucket that she'd borrowed from her little sister. One guy put in a quarter. The rest just walked away.

Then a huge, sudden rain almost drowned us. When TK ran inside the library, wet paper-towel wings stuck to his back. Laura yelled, "Keep chasing him, bat!"

She was the director, so in I went. Also, it was pouring rain, so I didn't need much convincing.

Mrs. Kent can be a helpful librarian, but she can also get a little grouchy. She crossed her arms and scowled, stopping TK in his tracks. And then I crashed into TK.

"Brubeck Ferrell, what is going on?" Mrs. Kent asked.

I wanted to point out that there were three of us dripping on her floor, so it was unfair to pick on just me. But I kept my mouth shut. Mrs. Kent and I have what Mom's girlfriend, Ginger, calls a "difficult relationship." And

I'm a total bookworm, so getting banned from the library would be the worst.

"We're trying to raise money so we can buy a bat detector for our Science Squad project," Laura explained while I wrung out my "wings."

Mrs. Kent sighed. "It's a noble cause, but you can't just barge in and disturb our patrons like this. Please rethink your strategy." As if to make up for shutting us down, she added, "You're always welcome here to use the computers and do research for your project. Just remember to consider the other patrons, please."

What could we do besides trudge home? It's not like we weren't already soaking wet. We had nothing but rainwater and one lousy quarter in our fundraising bucket. Clearly,

we'd need some other way to get money for our new bat-detection equipment.

When I got home, Mom saw I was dripping wet and immediately wrapped a giant towel around me. "You'll figure out a way to raise that money, Brubie."

Trust me, if anyone else on Earth called me Brubie, I'd clock them. But it gives me the warm fuzzies when Mom says it. And then she made me blackberry tea and poured it over a huge glass of ice. It was delicious. I'm reporting all this because her being so nice to me made me do something stupid. I asked the Forbidden Question.

"So, Mom, when are you and Ginger getting married?"

I've read the expression "her face fell" in a few books, but I had never seen it happen in real life. It was like gravity snuck up and pulled the smile out of Mom's cheeks.

"How many times have I explained this?" she asked.

"But—"

"No, you listen, Brubeck." Mom has unusually long index fingers, like magic wands, so when she holds one up, you shush. "Despite how common divorces are in this country, I think of marriage as forever. You know what else is forever?"

I'd heard this speech a bunch of times before, so I knew the answer. "Your being my mom is forever."

"That's right. I'm a mom first, always—before anything else in life."

"Can't you be my mom and Ginger's wife at the same time?"

She looked at me hard. Then a little bit of her smile came back. "Maybe when I'm convinced. When I'm absolutely sure that Ginger is as committed to being in your life as she is in mine."

In other words, no progress has been made on the marriage front. And I should learn to keep my trap shut.

The Bat-Detecting Project

Mr. Fong is such a goofball. You'd think a science nerd who's old like Mom would be all serious. But when we met in the Dolores Norton Middle School science room today to review the details of the Science Squad bat project, he was wearing plastic fangs. On his desk sat a big mosquito made of twisted wire. (Did Mr. Fong make that? Does he not have a life?)

As soon as we'd all taken our seats, he flapped his arms and pretended to fly around his desk. Then he scooped up the mosquito, turned it belly-up, and mimed biting its neck. Like a vampire that ran out of human corpses. It was kind of funny, but we all rolled our eyes and pretended it wasn't.

When he was done with his blood-sucking routine, Mr. Fong pulled the fangs out of his mouth. You could hear him slurping back strings of saliva. Ewww! "That Oscar-level performance," he said, "was to honor all of you who love science enough to set foot in the middle school during summer break. I salute you." He bowed, showing us the bald top of his head.

Then he got right down to business. "Just to review, this project is about acoustic monitoring. Your job is to help discover what kind of bats are in our region, based on their sounds. You'll all be listening to the bat calls using an ultrasound detector. Ideally, you'll also record them. Then you'll put the sound file into a database, logging in as much information as you have about the sound. Where and when you heard the sample are the most important things to report."

Laura's hand shot up, and she didn't wait until she was called on to start talking. "And what kind of bat it is."

Mr. Fong cocked his head and twisted his mouth. "Well, maybe. If you're really sure. Let me show you what the problem with that might be." He opened his laptop so we couldn't see the screen. "Listen to example one." He tapped a key. Squeaking and scraping sounds poured out of his little computer for a few seconds. "Now here's example two." More squeaking and scraping, a little louder and deeper than the first time. "Can you identify those different Wisconsin bats?"

We all started shouting out random species we'd heard of.

"Little brown."

"Big brown."

"Fruit bat."

"Indiana bat."

Mr. Fong held up his hands and we quieted down. "Fruit bats only live in warmer regions."

"I knew that," said Laura.

"Nevertheless, I believe we've proved my point. While it's great to listen closely to your recordings and try to tell them apart, it's harder than you might think to identify them. So, we'll let the bat experts who run the database identify the species for sure."

TK raised his hand. "Does it matter what kind of bats we find?"

Mr. Fong shook his head. "It's not that there are certain types you're supposed to find. The bat scientists just want information from your region of North America. They also like to compare data over time. For example, it seems that little brown bats are becoming less common. Anybody know why?"

I had a vague memory of reading something about this, so I raised my hand. "There's a disease, right?"

"Sadly, yes. White-nose syndrome. It's devastating the bat population. Please look it up when you get a chance, since it's very important to the study of bats these days."

"Can we take pictures of the bats?" Laura asked.

"Good question. Probably not a good idea. You'd need a flash, which can frighten them. So be sensitive to the bats' needs. Our job is to help them, right? Now, incredible as it may seem, I have things to do outside of this building during the summer. You kids stay here and talk about who's doing what."

Across Mr. Fong's desk, TK spread Mr. Fong's old-fashioned paper map of Garrett County, and Laura and I gathered around. "There should be plenty of places to try around here." With his index finger he traced a circle around the northeast part of our county, including the border where Ingotville Township meets Enderby Incorporated Village. All three of us live in that area.

Mr. Fong, who'd been gathering his belongings while we studied the map, spoke up. "I also need you three to run an important errand. You'll be representing Science

14

Squad, so I know I can count on you to be courteous and professional."

"Sir, yes sir," said Laura. She's been talking like that ever since her big brother joined the army. TK and I just said, "No problem."

"All right then." Mr. Fong handed TK a piece of paper with a name and address on it. "You're going to visit this gentleman, Mr. Pinter, preferably tomorrow. He owns an old bat detector that he's willing to lend us for this project."

"Oh, cool," we all said.

But the truth is, I wasn't so thrilled. We want a *good* bat detector. And we're going to raise the money to get it if it's the last thing we do.

Until then, I guess we'd better go see this Mr. Pinter over in Enderby. Not the way I wanted to spend tomorrow morning.

White-Nose Syndrome

The bat population is in danger. White-nose syndrome is a disease that is spreading quickly throughout North America and has started showing up in other parts of the world. This deadly fungus often appears as white powder on a bat's face. It makes the bats too sick to go out and search for food. The fungus grows in cool, wet places, so bats that live in caves are especially at risk. There is no cure yet, but scientists are trying to control the spread of the disease while they work on a vaccine.

Taking What We Can Get

No matter what else is wrong with my life, at least I don't live in Enderby. Nothing against the people there. It's just sort of an ugly town, at least compared to Ingotville. All the houses look the same: gray and small and sad.

Anyway, that's what TK and Laura and I thought when we biked over to Enderby this morning to see Mr. Pinter. Mom talked to Mr. Fong about him last night to make sure he's not an ax murderer or anything. She says he collects old scientific equipment and then lends it out to schools and clubs. Mr. Fong called him a generous eccentric. In other words, he's a little weird. But who isn't?

The main reason we didn't want to go was because we didn't want to be stuck with his junky old bat detector that he probably found at a flea market. We wanted a nice new one.

"What kind of detector do you think it will be?" TK asked in a panting voice while we pedaled up Jersey Road. All our parents had made us promise not to ride on County

Route 7 because there's no shoulder. And cars go fast. So
we had to deal with that torturous hill on Jersey Road. "Do
you think it's just one of those what's-it-called detectors?
Anodyne?"

Laura laughed between hard breaths. "You mean
heterodyne, TK. But who cares what kind it is? It probably
won't even work."

"Maybe we can give his old detector to the other kids,"
I said, feeling generous. "We'll use the new one."

Jersey Road finally flattened out, and TK stuck his legs
out as he coasted. "We don't have a new one yet, Bru. Who
knows? Maybe Mr. Pinter's detector is great."

Laura and I exchanged a "yeah, right" glance.

Like everybody else's house in Enderby, Mr. Pinter's
home was dull. The difference was, he had lots of stuff in
his yard. Antique stuff. On the way up his front walk we
passed one of those vintage bikes with the huge front wheel
and tiny back wheel. And TK pointed out a rusty porcelain
sink sitting in the grass.

"The sink belonged to Dr. Leon O. Jacobsen, the surgeon
who invented bone marrow transplants in 1949." That
nugget of information came from the bent-over man with

curly white hair who stood on the porch. Mr. Pinter waved at us. "You must be the kids from the science club."

"Yes, sir," said Laura, hurrying to the porch to shake his hand. TK and I hung back shyly. Laura introduced us all, and Mr. Pinter invited us in.

His house was dark and cluttered, but there wasn't much dust, and it smelled nice. Like burnt logs in the fireplace mixed with cinnamon.

"Sandalwood," TK said, sniffing the air.

"Good nose, my lad. Now, may I offer you fine young people some iced water and crackers?"

We took the water like we'd just been through the desert, but we politely refused the plate of plain dry saltines he held out. "Now, tell me about your bat project. I do love hearing youngsters talk about science."

We gave him all the details about what we were supposed to do, and why. I guess he noticed my eyes wandering over to the piles of odd equipment in what was probably supposed to be a living room. "Now, let me show you the detector you came for." He stood up with a struggle until TK steadied him. "Thank you. Such a gentlemanly fellow."

It took all of us to get the detector loose from the junk pile. I mean, the collection of important historical scientific thingamabobs. We had to move aside microscopes, a vintage X-ray machine (Mr. Pinter told us what that was), and a huge set of surgical tools wrapped in cloth. Finally Mr. Pinter pulled out a boxy rectangular device of ivory-colored plastic. It was about twice the size of his hand. A wrist strap was attached to one corner. It said "Echo Series D" at the top. The front featured four buttons, a pattern of small holes, and a sticker of a bat, which was peeling off on one wing.

Laura took the machine. I could tell she was forcing her nose not to wrinkle. "Could you please show us how it works, sir?"

Mr. Pinter's eyes sparkled when he answered. "How it works? Heavens, my dear, I have no idea. I just collect this equipment because I think it's neat. I don't know how to use it. I leave it to you scientists to figure it out."

We were already out of his neighborhood and back on Jersey Road before we all burst into laughter so hard that we had to get off our bikes. I did my best Mr. Pinter impression, making my voice hoarse. "I have no idea how to use it. I just think it's neat."

"What a wacky guy," said Laura.

"At least he was nice," said TK, pointing to his backpack, where he'd stashed the Echo Series D. "He says we can keep this as long as we want."

"Great," I said. "Lucky us."

"This is dumb," said Laura. She fidgeted with her handlebar streamers and wouldn't look at me. "Is this project even worth it?"

Laura's getting impatient. We'd better raise some money fast.

Weird but Pretty Music

The main reason I like going to TK's house is that his mom is such a character. Too bad his mom and dad fight so much that TK spends most of his time with his Uncle Morris.

Today his dad was out on a job, so TK was at his house. His mom answered the door and then crooked her fingers like claws. And she accented every other syllable, like in that old movie *Dracula*.

"Hel-LO, my DEAR. TaKWON is IN ze DEN." Kind of a dork. But a nice dork. And she also makes weird but tasty snacks. Today was Muenster cheese glued to little round crackers with a dot of barbecue sauce.

I have to admit I was a little annoyed at Laura for not coming. Yes, she has dance class on Wednesdays, but not until four. She could have come to TK's house before class. When I complained to TK, he gave her the benefit of the doubt, as usual.

"Maybe she has to prepare mentally before she dances. Maybe she doesn't like to eat before prancing around, and she knew Mom would serve up something."

I crossed my arms and stuck out my lower lip. "She's supposed to be part of our team. She doesn't seem very into it."

"But we still have each other. Come on, let's listen to some bats."

We were at TK's place because the library doesn't let you listen to the internet out loud, and there's only one headphone jack on each computer. So we were on TK's dad's computer. It's almost as old as TK.

"Is this even going to work?" I asked.

"It'll be fine." He poked my upper arm before using that finger to type a web address. On his phone, TK can write a thousand words a minute. On a computer keyboard, he might as well be jabbing letters with his nose. "There we go."

We were on batlisteners.com, which has a "field guide" of bat sounds.

"We need to learn how to tell the bats apart," said TK.

That seemed way too hard. "But Mr. Fong said we're not supposed to label the bat sounds," I said.

"No, he said we could try, but it was ultimately up to the experts. If we're going to do this project, let's try to do it all the way."

He was right. "Fine. But they're all going to sound the same."

"Won't know until we listen, Little Miss Negativity. Let's start with the hoary bat." He clicked on the first example. The background was just a hiss, but you could pick out high, quick chirps. "And here's the pocketed free-tail." This one chirped slower, at a slightly lower pitch. And a lot of its chirps were in sets of two. "Next up, Parnell's mustache bat."

"You made that up." But it was right there on the screen, a bat with reddish fur and pointy little gray ears. "What does it sound like?"

When TK pressed the play arrow, the room was filled with the highest-pitched chirping yet, in patterns of three, then one at a time, then three or four again. "See?" TK said. "Every bat sounds different. And check this out." He clicked a button, and a new page popped up. "Spectrograms."

"What does that mean?"

TK shrugged. "It says here that bat sounds are faster than 20 kilohertz, so they're considered ultrasound. And we can use imaging technology to make pictures of the sound patterns."

I leaned in closer to view a bunch of black squares decorated with red lines that formed squiggles and shapes. Each square was a spectrogram representing a particular bat sound. Some looked like capital letter L's, repeating over and over. Some looked almost like red fish in a black pond. Some spun up in spirals. A yellow dialogue box floated into view. "Is this sound Bat, Machine, or Insect?" it asked. "Want to learn more?"

We read the information: "When you record bats, your detector may pick up other sounds as well." It said bat sounds would show up higher on the spectrogram chart because they make the air vibrate so fast. Insects will be toward the bottom, with markings closer together than for the bats. And mechanical sounds like cars are also at the bottom, meaning lower hertz numbers, but uneven, without a pattern.

"I like listening to them better than looking at these spectrograms," I said. TK agreed, and went back to the sound field guide.

I think I was there for two hours. We read about the different ways bats use their calls. First they're for echolocation, where the bat sends out a sound and can tell where objects are based on how fast the sound comes back to its big ears. There are two types of echolocation calls: the kind sent over a larger distance, when they're searching for good insect-hunting areas, and another kind they use to find individual bugs to chomp on. There are also lower-frequency calls that bats use to talk to each other.

Ginger finally texted to ask when I would show up for dinner, so I told TK I had to go. But I can't stop thinking about the different types of cheeps and chirps and squeaks and pops, all different pitches and speeds. It was almost like music. I considered texting Laura that thought, but I wasn't sure she'd get it. We used to be able to read each other's minds. Now hers seems like it's written in invisible ink.

The Cutest Squeaks

Such a beautiful summer night! Laura and I spent it in the coolest possible way. Well, as cool as you can get when you're outside in the hot, humid air and not at the county pool.

It all started this afternoon, when Laura, TK, and I were at the library again, doing more research about where to find more bats.

"There are different places they might be," said TK. "Some types live in barns."

"The old Redmond place has some," said Laura. "I went over there once to sell cookies, and there were bats twirling around the porch light. I was a little freaked out, since this was before I got schooled by Science Squad. Mrs. Redmond just chuckled at them and shook her head. She said they must have a thousand or so in the barn."

"Barns. Check," I said. "Where else can we find them?"

TK read off the screen. "Trees, caves."

"Do we have any caves around here?" Laura asked. "Second question: don't bears also live in caves? And third question: am I going to get eaten by a bear while I'm doing this project?"

I laughed as I answered her questions in order. "Don't know, I think so, and I hope so."

She scribbled a frownie face on my spiral notebook. "Bet you get eaten first."

"Actually, I bet *I* will," said TK. "I probably taste the best." He pointed at something on the computer. "Don't know about caves, you guys, but here's something we definitely have in Ingotville."

Looking over his shoulder, I read aloud from the paragraph he was pointing to. "'Some species of bats will make their homes in abandoned mines.'"

I clapped my hands. "Mines we've got. We are set!"

"Seriously? Abandoned mines?" whined Laura. "Aren't they gross and creepy? And I might twist my ankle and never be able to dance again."

Her attitude really bothered me, but TK laughed it off. "Wear sensible shoes and shine a flashlight on the ground. Anyway, sometimes you have to get a little dirty to do real science."

"What he said," I agreed. I tried to smile at Laura, but I wasn't feeling it. She used to be fun and up for anything.

Mrs. Kent poked her head around the YA nonfiction bookcase. "Although I am pleased by your enthusiasm for your science project, this does remain a functioning library. We have story time going on right now." And the head disappeared.

"Let's go," TK said, handing me my pencil, which had rolled toward him across the table. "I have to get over to Uncle Morris's anyway."

Outside the library we made a plan: Laura and I would go over to the abandoned iron ore mines and try to figure out if there were any bats—and if so, where they lived.

"We can try Mr. Pinter's detector," Laura suggested.

The second that idea left her lips, TK jumped in front of her on the sidewalk with his arms out like a monster. "No way. I have to help my uncle tonight. Don't you dare go detecting without me. Or you'll pay the price!" He roared a couple times, but TK is so sweet that it just made Laura and me giggle.

"We'll do recon," said Laura, once again talking like she's in the army. "And report back."

I saluted. "Yes, sir."

Later that afternoon, the two of us biked to the north side of town, then over County Route 7 and across the field. The holes where mine workers used to go in were boarded up with wooden slats. "Do not enter" signs were posted everywhere. Laura got off her bike and stared. "How can the bats get in and out, do you think?"

Since we didn't have binoculars, I used my phone's camera to zoom in on the nearest mine entrance. "Those boards are old and rotten. And there are lots of gaps and holes in the rock. Little bats can fly out of there with no problem, I bet."

There was something silencing about the moment when the sun set. We settled onto the ground, side by side, watching the sky darken.

Then I saw them. "Bats," I whispered. They flew out of every crevice like a magical black potion overflowing. Swarms of them. Impossible to count. I swear I heard all their tiny wings flapping like gentle rain on leaves. And the squeaking and chirping was so adorable!

"I thought we wouldn't be able to hear them," said Laura quietly. "Aren't they supposed to be ultrasonic?"

"The sounds they use for echolocation are ultrasonic," I whispered. "That's what we'll be recording, I guess."

Even in the dim light, I could see Laura was frowning. "What's wrong?" I asked.

She just shrugged.

"Don't you think this is perfect?" I asked. "We're going to get all kinds of stickers for this bat project, since we have access to these mines."

"Yeah, I guess." She looked at the snaking line of tiny bats silhouetted against the day's last light. Instead of sighing in contentment at all that natural beauty, she wrinkled her nose and stood up.

"Don't tell me you don't like bats," I said. "Not after everything we've learned about them."

"No, bats are fine. It's just, these bats are so ordinary. Little brown bats probably, the most common type in Wisconsin." She raised the kickstand on her bike and pushed it back toward the field. I followed.

Laura said, "I want to record special bats, like maybe the eastern red. Wouldn't it be cool to be the first citizen scientist in our region to record an eastern red bat?"

I didn't know what to say. Bats are bats. I thought we were trying to help all the species. But I didn't bother to say that to Laura.

Best Idea Ever!

Things are looking up! I met Mom for lunch at the Wagon Spokes Café. She had a salad the size of the *Titanic*. (How does her body process all those greens?) I had my usual: cucumber, watercress, and cream cheese with caramelized onions on thick multigrain toast. Y-u-u-m-m-m!

Corinne, that nice older woman with the curly hair, was our server, and she really wanted us to have dessert. When Mom said no thanks (I didn't get a vote), Corinne tried to change our minds. "Are you sure? We have mile-high apple pie with a scoop of cinnamon ice cream. There's deep chocolate layer cake with hot fudge filling. How about strawberries and sponge cake cubes in a bowl of vanilla whipped cream?"

"We try to avoid eating added sugar," said Mom.

Me? I was grabbing the underside of the tabletop for dear life. "No, thank you." I forced myself to say.

But what Corinne said next was like a reward for my self-control. "I heard you and your friends are raising money for birdwatching?"

"We don't watch birds. We listen to bats."

Her face froze for a second, but she recovered quickly. "Oh. Well. Anyway, I wanted to suggest that you have a bake sale. You could make cupcakes and decorate them with birds. I mean bats." She shook her head slightly, like she was thinking *Who would want to study bats?* She went on, "I bet I could even convince Chef Tracy to share her Birthday Bash Cupcake recipe."

"No way!" In my excitement, I tipped over my water glass. Mom, who has Spidey senses, zapped her hand across the table and steadied it. Grinning at my clumsiness, I said, "That would be so great, Corinne. Birthday Bash Cupcakes are legendary. You think Tracy would really tell us the recipe?"

She winked. "For girls trying to get a better education, there is nothing Tracy won't do."

While Corinne went into the kitchen to talk to Tracy, I promised Mom up and down that I would only *make* the cupcakes, not eat them. Her face suddenly looked really soft and warm. "You're welcome to have one. And I'll pay for the ingredients so it doesn't cut into your profit." That, right there, is sweeter than a Birthday Bash Cupcake.

So, here I am with Chef Tracy's recipe. She let me take a photo of the worn, stained piece of paper it's scribbled on. I made a list of all the groceries we need for four dozen cupcakes, which doubled the recipe. Ginger reminded me to be super careful to double every single ingredient, or the whole recipe will tank. "Baking is all about chemistry and physics," she said.

That's all right. I like science. I'm ready. TK and Laura will be over after lunch tomorrow to help make them. This is going to be epic!

Bat Adaptations

Bats are not blind. But because they need to get around in the dark, they have some special adaptations to take the place of seeing. They make sounds with their larynx or nose. Others click their tongues. They use their big ears for echolocation. The sounds bats send out bounce back, and that helps them determine how far away objects are. This keeps them from bumping into things as they fly and tells them where to find insects. Bats also use sounds for communicating with one another, but these are often at lower frequencies.

Fundraising Flop No. 2

Maybe I should just stay up here in my room for the rest of my life. Mom and Ginger can leave food and library books outside my door. I won't bother anybody or mess anything else up ever again.

I guess I'd better write down what happened today. Not that it will make me feel better. I'm not sure I'll ever feel better. But it's too ridiculous to believe, so I really should record the details for future historians. File this under "stupidest girl in the world." Or at least in Wisconsin.

The prep for the bake sale was going so well. Mom and Ginger took me to the grocery store together, like it was a fun family outing. Me and my two moms. Maybe someday I can call them that for real.

I looked at the photo of Chef Tracy's recipe on my phone and called out ingredients as we walked through the aisles.

When Ginger split off to get some sugar, I said to Mom, "I think we have four eggs at home."

"Better buy more anyway, just in case." See? We were being so careful.

"You guys, we need these!" Ginger came bounding back and tossed a bunch of clear plastic bags into our cart. They were full of little black bats on sticks that you were supposed to poke into cakes. "I found them in a bargain bin," she said. "Long time since Halloween. They must have been waiting for us to come buy them."

"Perfect!" I said.

"Perfect," Mom agreed.

Everything about life seemed perfect. Oh, I wish the rest of the day had gone that well.

Right after lunch, TK and Laura came over as agreed upon. TK volunteered to get our bake sale table ready. When he was a little kid, his arm got a nasty burn in the kitchen. He has a scar shaped like a Viking oar on his forearm. So, he bowed out of the actual baking. But Laura and I could see him out in the yard through the window, unfolding bright yellow tablecloths. He also taped a big "Buy a Cupcake for Science" sign to the power poles for blocks around, featuring our address and cartoonish arrows.

"There are tons of yard sales in this neighborhood today," he reported when he got back from taping up signs.

"I hope four dozen cupcakes are enough to feed all those treasure-hunters."

Laura shook her head and put one hand on her hip. "It's not enough. Let's make it five dozen."

"We only have four cupcake pans, though," I pointed out. Two we'd dug out from the back of our kitchen cabinet. And Grandma Farrell lent us two. She is an excellent baker. She even let us use her pure Madagascar vanilla extract—Tracy's recipe insists that no other kind will do—so we wouldn't have to buy a new bottle.

"We can't spend any more time searching for pans. Guess we'll have to stick with just four dozen," I said sadly to Laura.

"Or not." She pranced over to the rolling carry-on suitcase she'd brought over. Do I even need to mention that it was pink and covered with tiny cartoon cats? After a few seconds of rummaging, she pulled out a cupcake pan! "I thought I should bring it, just in case." She batted her eyelashes.

I gave her a hug. "You are the best."

"I know, right?"

So, we were all set to make sixty cupcakes. Like a math genius, I figured out how to increase the ingredients to make that many. Bump everything up by 25 percent. So, the four cups of flour became five. The three teaspoons of salt grew to 3 3/4. The quarter-cup of cornstarch . . . that took some thinking. Then I got it: a quarter-cup equals four tablespoons. So increasing by 25 percent became five tablespoons. Anyway, the same math went for everything in the recipe. I broke into that extra dozen eggs. Thanks, Mom!

This might sound strange, but we were excited about the cornstarch. It was the secret ingredient for a "silky, springy cake," according to Chef Tracy.

Laura's job was to operate the mixer and keep scraping the sides of the bowl. I dumped the ingredients in, one by one. It's possible I was so proud and confident that my math was right, I may have let my attention lag for a second. *Just* a second.

With everything in the bowl starting to blend together, Laura pushed the lever on the mixer up to number three. The blades purred like a helicopter. Our precious bat-batter turned smooth and sleek.

"All ready," said Laura. "I put the cupcake liners in the pans and preheated the oven, so we are good to go."

She filled three cupcake pans and I filled two, stopping the mound of sweet, beige batter two-thirds from the top of each liner, just like Chef Tracy advised. We have a very wide oven, so we could put three pans on the top rack and two on the bottom.

This seems so easy. That thought should have been a warning. Nothing is ever that easy for me. But I was just so excited . . .

While the cupcakes baked, Laura waited in the kitchen for the oven buzzer to ring. "I'll make the chocolate frosting and get the plastic bat sticks out of the packages," she said like an army general rallying her troops. "You go out and see how TK's doing with the table. Oh, hang on!" She ran to her suitcase and pulled out a gray metal box, about the size of a gaming console. "This is for cash. My dad put in a bunch of one-dollar bills to get us started making change."

"That's so sweet!" I grabbed the box and ran out to help TK put the finishing touches on the table and signs. Our neighbor from across the street, Mrs. Finley, came over to see what we were up to. Before I knew it, nineteen minutes had passed, and I heard the kitchen buzzer through the screen door.

Inside, it smelled like vanilla heaven. But Laura's stony face made it seem like she was in the opposite of heaven.

In one hand she held the scrap of paper that we had done the math on to make the recipe bigger. "I checked the numbers. Everything was correct. What could have happened?" She was speaking like a robot with no emotion.

TK and I followed her horrified gaze to the five cupcake pans on the counters. Instead of fluffy cupcakes, we had sixty cupcake liners that were two-thirds full of hard, golden-brown nuggets. "What could have happened?" Laura repeated.

"They didn't rise," said TK. "Did you guys put in the baking powder?"

"Yes," Laura and I snapped at the same time.

"You're sure?" He showed us the little yellow canister marked baking powder. It was still sealed.

"Oh, my gosh," I said, pressing my forehead against Laura's shoulder. "We were so excited about the cornstarch, Tracy's secret ingredient. And it looks just like baking powder, in a yellow package. And they're listed right next to each other on the recipe."

"So, you didn't put the leavening in," said Laura. "You made a whole bunch of bricks." She breathed in through her nose. "Sixty vanilla bricks that we can't possibly sell. Congratulations, Bru."

You know what's even more annoying than ruined cupcakes? The fact that Laura got all snooty about it. Like she blamed me, even though she was standing right there when I put in the ingredients. What's her problem?

TK went back out to take down all his signs. Laura and I barely spoke to each other while we cleaned up the kitchen and yard. And we haven't even texted each other tonight, which never happens.

It was a bake sale tragedy for the ages. I just hope it's not the end of my friendship with Laura too.

The Echo Series D

A good night's sleep must have swept away the disappointment of yesterday's cupcake catastrophe.

First thing this morning TK texted: "Bat detecting tonight, right?" In five minutes flat, we had a plan to meet at the stoplight on County Route 7 after supper.

Nobody could say we weren't prepared. Besides Mr. Pinter's bat detector, we each had a flashlight, bug spray, a bottle of water, and about a week's worth of granola bars. Once we'd crossed the road and were getting ourselves organized to hike across the field to the mine entrance, TK held up his water bottle. "To teamwork."

"To saving the bats," said Laura, clicking her bottle against his.

I reached into my backpack blindly, pulled something out, and toasted with the bottle of bug spray. "Together forever to save the bats."

We had sort of figured out how the detector worked, but Laura wanted to test it before the bats emerged from the rocks. Once we'd reached the scrubby, flat area in front of the mines, she asked TK to let her hold it. "The video I saw online said to set the frequency at 45 kilohertz, and then rub your fingers together near it."

"And that does what, exactly?" TK asked.

Laura shrugged. "I forget. Let's find out. Bru, you do the buttons and I'll do the fingers." She handed me Mr. Pinter's detector.

I turned the machine on by using my thumb to rotate a small wheel on the side. Then I hit the button marked "Frequency" and turned the side wheel again until it said 45 kilohertz. When I nodded at Laura, she rubbed her thumb against her index finger about a foot from the microphone holes.

The craziest sound came out, like two balloons scraping together. "That's it?" Laura asked, frowning. "I thought it would sound amazing. This sounds like an otter singing underwater."

"I would pay top dollar to hear an otter singing underwater," I said. But Laura just shrugged and turned away.

"This is going to be an unusual experience," TK said, laughing. "Did you know that little brown bats emit with the same intensity as a smoke alarm?"

"Really? That's cool!" I said.

We sat for a moment. "Now what do we do?" TK looked at me, as if I might know.

"I guess we wait for the bats."

Our research recommended a frequency setting of 40,000 hertz to pick up the sounds of little brown bats. I turned the dial a little, to 40 kilohertz, and the machine was ready to go.

They say waiting is the hardest part. They're not kidding. We knew we shouldn't have any sound or bright lights coming from our phones, so we turned them off. That made the time until dusk go even slower. At one point we sang "Row, row, row your boat" as a three-part round. Then Laura pointed out that the bats might not be enjoying our concert, so we stopped.

Finally, the sky in the west started to turn pink, and the mine's rocky face glowed. TK balled his fists and tensed his muscles. "There they are," he whispered.

I clicked our machine on and held it up. The bats came out of the rocks and swooped around us. I'm not sure I breathed more than ten times in those first few minutes. I swear we could hear the flapping and whooshing of their wings, and a lot of chattering. It's hard to believe that most of the sounds they use for echolocation are ultrasonic, so we humans can't hear them. Imagine how noisy they sound to each other!

It was kind of eerie to concentrate on how dark it was getting. But exciting too. The bats trickled out at first, and then they swarmed. I've read that some bats come out of caves in a big cyclone shape. But these guys were doing lots of little spirals all over the rock face and then flying off like black butterflies against the gray-blue sky.

Some flew over us, and some went into Decker Woods next to the mine. We had a pair of headphones, which I plugged into the bat detector and pulled over my ears. I was expecting all kinds of interesting squeaks and blurps and clicks. All I got was static. I tried moving the volume up and down. I tried changing the frequency. Nothing but distortion, like a librarian saying "Shhh!" inside my brain.

I turned the knob a little more and walked closer to the edge that overlooked the mine entrance. TK put his arms around me to make sure I didn't fall. Finally it worked—a few little squeaks and blips that sounded like they were supposed to sound. And then back to static. I pulled the headphones off in disgust.

"Let me try," said Laura, as if she were some kind of mechanical genius. Of course, it didn't go any better for her, and she threw the headphones on the ground. TK gave it a try, but it was the same bunch of nothing for him.

"Well," I said, "at least we got a few seconds of real bat sounds."

"Enough of a recording to put it in the database?" Laura asked.

"Wait. What recording?" TK looked at the front, side, and back of the detector, and asked a question we should have asked a couple days ago. "Can this thing even make recordings?"

So, long story short, we have a bat detector that barely works at all, and it doesn't make recordings anyway. Oh boy, do we need one of these fundraisers to bring in the big bucks!

Types of Bat Detectors

Humans cannot hear most bat sounds because the frequencies are too high. Bat detectors lower the frequencies so we can hear them.

The most common and least expensive kind of bat detector is heterodyne. You must choose the frequency for the type of bats you expect to hear. In general, smaller bats echolocate at higher frequencies.

Frequency division detectors record a large range of frequencies all at once. You can hear different types of bats at the same time, but they're harder to tell apart than with a heterodyne detector.

A time expansion detector is usually very expensive. It makes a digital recording of the bats, then plays it back ten or twenty times slower. It's the best possible sound quality, but you have to wait to listen until after the recording is made. The other types of detectors work in real time.

The Story of a Caterpillar

This equipment situation is so frustrating. For a few minutes last night, I actually thought about quitting Science Squad. But I shouldn't give up, right? And Science Squad can be really fun. Mr. Fong gave a great presentation about bats when we first decided on the detection project. He showed us a computer simulation of how the ultrasound works. How it's *supposed* to work, I should say. This is making me upset again, so I'm going to change the subject.

Happier topic: how I got into Science Squad.

Last school year, sixth grade, we had this great science teacher named Ms. Steinberg. She was hilarious, and so smart. One day when Laura and I were in the cafeteria at lunch, we noticed a caterpillar crawling across the table. The classic pale green kind with yellow and black stripes.

"It looks like it chewed its way out of the pages of *Alice in Wonderland*," I said. And this will sound stupid, but it seemed friendly, so I started petting it with my index finger.

"Don't, it's poisonous!"

Laura and I turned to find out who'd said that. It was Ms. Steinberg! Since I was busy having a heart attack over almost dying, Laura was the first one to speak up. "That cute little guy is poisonous?"

Ms. Steinberg was always a clown, like she was in a sitcom going for laughs. But it was never annoying because she is actually cool and super nice. She is also short and wide, with pretty much no neck, so she makes me think of Ginger.

Laura asked again. "Is it really dangerous?"

Ms. Steinberg shrugged. Not a normal shrug, but exaggerated, holding her shoulders right up against her ears and bending her knees, like somebody was pressing her whole body down. "Hey, I don't know. Do you know?" she asked.

When Laura and I shook our heads, Ms. Steinberg lunged toward the table, catching herself with both hands between my sandwich and Laura's hot lunch tray. She whispered really loud, "Would you like to find out more about this wiggly little weirdo?"

"Yeah!" Laura and I said at the same time.

"Then here you go." Like a magician, Ms. Steinberg was suddenly holding a flier for the Science Squad. "Check it out." Then she spun around and bounced away. When she reached the end of our table, she called back. "That's a monarch caterpillar. Probably escaped from the eighth-grade cocoon experiment. Not poisonous, but please don't touch. It has more important things to worry about than some human poking at it."

Laura used the brochure to gently scoop up the caterpillar and carry him to a window, which was open just enough to let him out. We read the brochure and applied for Science Squad that afternoon. The rest is history.

I suppose Ms. Steinberg would have made a great stand-up comedian, but I'm glad she's a teacher. I miss her, even though Mr. Fong is nice. We'll have him next school year, which is fine because I'm happy to be done with sixth grade!

Common Bats of North America

There are dozens of bat species living in North America and over a thousand worldwide. All the North American ones are microbats (small species). Almost all are insectivores. Here are ten of the most common types of North American bat:

Big brown bat
Little brown bat
Eastern red bat
Brazilian free-tail bat
Hoary bat
Evening bat
Silver-haired bat
Pallid bat
Northern long-eared myotis
Eastern pipistrelle

The BatSong 4000

You know what's really dangerous? Fantasy-shopping. When you go online and shop for exactly what you would buy if you had all the money in the world. Sure, it's fun for a while. But then it gets super depressing as the reality sinks in that you'll never be able to buy whatever it is.

TK and I got a harsh reminder of that today. We met up at the library to look at bat detectors online. At first it was nice and reasonable.

"Here's a decent heterodyne detector for $44," said TK. "It's basically like Mr. Pinter's, only new. So, I assume it would work better."

"But we'd need new headphones too," I said. "If you can't really monitor what you're getting, there's no point."

We did a quick look for headphones. Of course, you can get a pair of earbuds for $12. But we wanted something really nice that blocks out all the other sounds. "Let's find one that makes you feel like you're one with the bats." TK does get poetic sometimes.

The headphones we liked best were definitely more than twelve bucks. Like, fifteen times more. Oops.

This stuff just snowballs. Once we'd convinced ourselves that only the best headphones would do, TK took the next step into the Desert of Financial Hopelessness. "We have to find a way to record these sounds."

I tried to be the adult. "A little recorder can't be that much."

"Girl, get serious. We need high-quality recordings, so the experts who run the database can be sure what kind of bats we've got around here. Solid data, you know? That will really impress the judges once we get to the National Science Squad Conference." He turned to me fiercely. "Which we *will*."

"Of course we will. And you're absolutely right. Let's see what kinds of recorders are out there."

Who knew that an "environmental recorder" was even a thing? A very, very expensive thing. We found a fancy-looking one called the Plektron 14.2. For a cool $450 you get a little machine that can record at different speeds, play back at different speeds, make four different formats of sound files, change pitch, and plug into your phone, laptop, or detector.

"Will it vacuum the house too?" I wondered.

"That's extra," TK said with a laugh. "But seriously, we have to get this. We need this recorder."

"Yes. Yes." An important, sobering thought came over me. "And TK?"

"Yeah?"

"If we're bothering to get the best headphones and the best recorder, you know what else we need to do?"

"I'm pretty sure I know where you're going with this, but I want to hear you say it."

"We need to up our game with the detector. Heterodyne is not good enough."

"That's what I'm talking about!" TK pumped his fist in the air. "Only the best, baby." He screwed up his face. "Are we looking for a frequency division detector?"

"Not sure." I did a quick search. I came up with a good blog post about bat detectors on an Australian wildlife website. "This says that, in some ways, frequency division is better than heterodyne because it self-tunes the frequency to any kinds of bats that happen to be in the area."

"As opposed to . . ."

"As opposed to heterodyne, where you have to tune in to a particular bat's frequency."

TK nodded. "This sounds promising."

"But there's a problem," I went on. "Frequency division ones don't focus on one bat at a time, so it can be harder to tell the bats apart."

"Not good. Let's go upscale." He took over the keyboard, entering the search term "time expansion detector." Bullseye. "Brubeck, I'd like you to meet the BatSong 4000." He paused to read and then sighed. "I think I'm in love."

The BatSong 4000. It's called a time expansion detector because it literally slows down the sound waves it picks up, so you get the clearest possible recording. This one lets you choose between ten or twenty times slower. Plus it comes with a heterodyne function, in case you want to listen in real time. And it costs $600. Ha ha ha! Oh, boy.

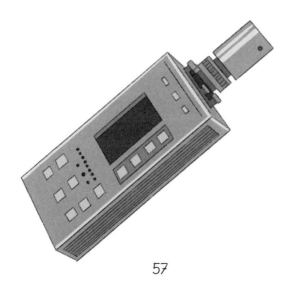

With the recorder, that adds up to over a thousand buckaroos. Not gonna happen. But wow, it would be so great if we could get killer equipment like we saw today.

I came home feeling worse than ever about our Science Squad project. Maybe Laura's right to wonder whether this is all worth it.

I need to shift my thinking. The bats need us!

Fundraising Flop No. 3

Today I officially proved I'm a chicken. And not as committed to raising money as I thought I was. I also learned not to tell Laura when I do online fantasy-shopping. She has trouble distinguishing that from reality.

Laura skidded into our driveway on her bike this morning and beeped the pink horn on her pink handlebars. The one shaped like a hedgehog, because for the past few months, everything has to be cute. "Kawaii" is her favorite new word since she found out it means "extra-cute" in Japanese. To be honest, all that kawaii is driving me a little nuts.

As soon as I showed up at the screen door, she said, "We're going for the big bucks." She pointed to the hills behind my house. "Let's ask that guy."

I turned to look. Nothing but ash trees. "I don't see anybody."

From the bottom of her kitty-shaped backpack, she pulled out the tiniest pair of binoculars I'd ever seen. "The mansion," she said, offering me the binoculars. But I didn't need them. I knew what the mansion looked like. It's hard to see through the summer leaves, but in winter that big, white house stares down on our little mint-green house. The windows look like eyes, and it seems like it's judging how little our house is.

"That's just a phony McMansion," Mom said when I pointed out its size one day. "It can't hurt us."

I tried to get Ginger to laugh at the name Phony McMansion, but she just squinted up at it and smiled in a weird, secretive way. I'm not sure what she was thinking about.

Anyway, Laura decided we needed to ride our bikes up to Phony McMansion and ask Mr. Rich to help pay for our new detecting equipment.

"We can't just waltz up to the door and say, 'Hey, how about some money for Science Squad?'"

"People ask rich folks to donate money all the time," said Laura. "Don't worry. I'll do the talking."

"Well, I guess we could try." I wasn't crazy about this plan, but I had no idea what else we could do to raise money. "Let's call TK. He can meet us at the county road."

"Girls only." Laura pulled her helmet over her long, black hair. "Girls seem more trustworthy. I read that on the internet."

"Okaaay, then." I didn't mention that the internet also says you can regrow cut off fingers if you take certain vitamins. And that the Earth is flat. The internet is full of nonsense.

But I went along with the plan. It was nice to spend some time alone with Laura.

The air felt thick and hot, but I appreciated the wide clouds. They looked like what Ms. Steinberg calls altostratus, casting big shadows over the hillside. That made an uphill bike ride seem like less of a leg-killer.

On the way I asked, "What do we say to this guy? Or lady? Do we know their name?"

Laura panted as she fought her way up the incline. "R. Chen. That's what it says on the mailbox."

"Mailbox? You've already gone up there?"

"More recon." If Laura ever decides to join the army, she'll volunteer for every recon job. "Here's my idea. Once we get up there, we knock on the door and say, 'Hey, Mr. or Ms. Chen! We're two girls in Science Squad, and would you like to donate to our project about bats?'"

"At which point they hand us a $10 bill and wish us luck." I slowed my pedaling and let Laura pull ahead. "You know we need about a thousand dollars, right? Maybe let's wait until we've planned a really good presentation to impress this Chen person."

"Spontaneous is better," Laura called back. "We'll speak from the heart. Too late to turn around, Bru. We're here."

The newly paved turnoff from the main road was marked "Private." A large silver mailbox was labeled "R.

Chen." Oh, and a big metal gate blocked the entrance a few yards down the little road.

"You never went up to the house, did you?" I asked, my heart pounding from all that biking. "This is as far as we're allowed."

"No, it's fine." But her voice strained from nerves. And five seconds after she started up that private road toward the gate, we heard barking in the distance—deep barking, like from a huge dog. It was heading our way.

We didn't slow down enough to talk until we reached the bottom of the hill. So much for getting a wealthy patron to buy us our new bat detector. It's just too nerve-wracking.

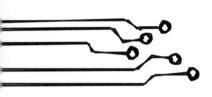

The BatWrong -5000

Ginger is so sweet!

I was reading on the front porch after lunch, and the UPS guy pulled up. He had a box addressed to Ginger. When I brought it inside to her, I asked if it had to do with her music. "No, I think it has more to do with *your* music."

She had me stand there while she opened the box on the kitchen table. Inside the outer box was a smaller box wrapped in plastic. She handed it to me. "Care to do the honors?"

I ripped off the packaging and just stared. The box said, "DIY Bat Detector." I had no clue what to say. So thoughtful, but so laughable, considering that amazing time expansion detector TK and I are now obsessing over. I'd told Ginger about that last night, and I guess she immediately went online and ordered this kit with one-day delivery. Sweet but hopeless.

Obviously, since I'm not a creep, I didn't tell Ginger that I thought her gift was lame. "Thank you so, so much!" I said, giving her a big hug.

"Glad you like it. Let's go build it."

"Um." This was not how I had planned to spend my afternoon. And besides the fact that I knew it would be a waste of time for a couple non-mechanics to try to build some sorry excuse for a detector, there was another issue. "Don't you have a deadline? Aren't you supposed to be composing music right now?"

The look she gave me is hard to describe. Part annoyed, part guilty, part amused, part feisty. All she said was, "We have the tools we need in the garage."

So, we spent a kind of insane afternoon in the garage, building a bat detector! Turns out it's not totally do-it-yourself. A bunch of tiny electronics were already attached to a circuit board. Using glue and a soldering iron (who knew we have a soldering iron?!), we had to attach an ultrasound microphone, two knobs, some wires, some round metal doo-hickeys called "potentiometers" that control the voltage, a speaker, a thing that you can snap a battery onto, and some things called "electrolytic capacitators," which I think sound like an ingredient in a sports drink.

SCIENCE SQUAD

The good news is, there were detailed instructions with lots of pictures. The bad news is, neither of us had ever done anything like this before. I memorized this line from the instructions because I read it so many times: "If the device does not work, use a magnifying glass to check all the connections and soldering."

Finally, we got it to respond when I rubbed my fingers in front of the microphone. The way we cheered, you'd have thought we had cured cancer or something.

I'm calling our masterpiece the BatWrong –5000 because it's totally the opposite of the bat detector I expected to have at this point. Ginger was so exhausted afterward that she went straight in to take a nap and slept right through dinner! I don't know if this thing will be any good for detecting bats, but it was sure nice to spend that much time with her.

10 Things I Love about Ginger

A list for Mom (maybe I'll show to her someday . . .)

1. She calls me Jazz.

2. She writes music for video games, which is the coolest job I've ever heard of.

3. Her name is Ginger, but she dyes her hair the color of red wine. Rebel!

4. She likes bats, bugs, and reptiles.

5. Once when I skinned my knee, she drove me all the way to Miller's Pharmacy so we could get Wonder Woman bandages.

6. She seems so comfortable in the old green armchair, like she belongs there. Which she does.

7. She has a weird sense of humor. Once TK and I were stuck on a math problem. Ginger said, "Studies show that four out of three people are bad at fractions." It took us like five minutes to get that. Classic Ginger.

8. I'm not supposed to tell you this, Mom, but Ginger started an online savings account to help with my college costs. She puts in a little bit every time she gets paid for a job, so I'll have enough there in a few years to pay for books and stuff.

9. Cheddar cheese. She knows it doesn't belong on a pizza, but it's awesome on a burger.

10. She loves you, Mom, and you love her. That's the best thing of all.

Why Bat Detecting Is Important

Collecting bat sounds is a way to keep track of the population of different species in different areas of the world. If a species is not detected as often as it used to be, that could mean the population in a certain area has dropped. Bat scientists use this information to look for changing climate, problems with food supply, and disease. Where bats are struggling, there are often general problems with the environment. Scientists estimate that only 5 percent of the world's bat species have ever been recorded, which is why data collection by citizen scientists is so important to provide information about which bats live where.

Light Rescuer!

Dum-dum-da-DEEEE-dum! Ginger wrote that victory tune, and I cannot get it out of my head. The sound of victory! I spent all afternoon with TK at his Uncle Morris's house, playing video games. Well, *the* video game—*Light Rescuer.* The main theme she composed is very catchy, and it really gets your blood pumping, like you're a hero.

Ginger wrote the music for that game at the beginning of last year, and yesterday, she finally got a login we could use to play it. Part of how they pay her—besides with money, obviously—is a lifetime subscription to any game she writes the music for.

The downside: when her deadline for turning in the music for a game gets close, she goes into high-stress mode. And guess what? I heard her telling Mom this morning (I may have been spying outside their closed door) that the music for the second *Light Rescuer* game is due in five weeks. That sounds like a long time to me, but the way she said "Five. Weeks." was as tense as a rubber band stretched around a hundred pens. "And nothing is working," she added. Then I heard the *thump*, like she had thrown a shoe across the room. "Roger's going to fire me."

"Roger's not going to fire you, sweetheart," Mom said. "You're brilliant, and you'll get this done. You always do."

At that point I heard one of them coming near the door, so I scooted down the hallway. But I'd better be careful when dealing with Ginger for the rest of the summer. The super-stressful days are coming!

Anyway, back to the game. TK and I sat at his uncle's computer and opened the tutorial. He immediately pointed at the most spectacular character, a blue-skinned woman with an eagle head and long arms that never stopped waving. Her full-length black dress was studded with purple jewels. "Ra-Fu, Queen of Darkness." He said the character's name like he already worshiped her. Count on TK to identify with the charismatic evil ones.

"She is our enemy, TK," I told him. "And see? She has really powerful weapons to use against us. Like those jewels on her dress can erase your memory if she throws one at you. And she can blow a temporal cloud from her evil lungs that can stop time or move it forward or backward."

"Nasty, but oh, so cool! And who is this interesting brother?" TK rolled the cursor over a brown-skinned male character. His name was Sep. He wore a long green velvet robe, and his description made me cringe as TK read it: "Sep is the queen's consort, but they don't always get along. Spoiled and wishy-washy, unreliable, unpredictable. When you cross his path, you can't guess whether he'll be representing the Queen of Darkness or be miffed at her and ready to give you state secrets."

"That idiot's going to be a problem," I growled.

The concept of *Light Rescuer* is that Queen Ra-Fu has captured Light. Light can only send out a few rays from its prison cell, but the player's job is to rescue Light (hence the name of the game) by performing tasks. Each task you complete disintegrates ten bricks in the prison wall. So you get more light and other strengths each time.

TK created an avatar named Windspear. Mine is Swifthorse, a woman wearing a tunic made of the swirling dreams of running horses. So magical! Do not mess with Swifthorse. She's going to save Light, I promise you. We only got to Level 2, but we have the rest of the summer to finish it.

P. S. Ginger's music is super awesome. She even got some of it recorded by a whole symphony orchestra!

Booooooo!

In It for the Wrong Reason

It's been a weird afternoon. Laura texted TK and me to meet her at the library "to talk bats!" I was pretty pumped about this, since Laura hasn't seemed that enthusiastic about Science Squad lately. I was hoping she had read an article or seen a video that really inspired her.

Even though I pedaled so fast that my legs burned, TK was already locking up his bike when I braked along the side of the library. He gave me a big grin and a thumbs up, and in we went.

There was Laura, perched on a stool, her face pushed an inch from the computer screen. Her hair was in a bun, held together with a pink stick that looked like a skewer. Since when does she do up her hair? I almost teased her about it but changed my mind.

With her finger, she traced a line from left to right along the screen. I could tell she was studying a chart. And liking what she found there. Oh, and talking to herself.

74

"Nope, nope. Awesome. There's one. That's Michigan. Doesn't count. And nope." *Suddenly she swung around with a maniacal gleam in her eye.* "It's ours. It's all ours!"

"Dang it, girl," *TK said.* "We didn't even think you knew we were here."

With both hands, Laura pointed to various places on her skull. "Eyes everywhere. I see everything. Pauline says that's why I'm so good at turns." *Pauline is Laura's ballet teacher, who's somewhere between that Wakandan princess and Princess Leia in Laura's estimation.* "Come, come, guys. Have a look-see."

TK laughed. "Look-see. You sound like my grandma." *The three of us jostled for a view of the screen. It showed a chart with bat species along the left margin. Different regions in North America labeled the columns across the top.*

"This is the database log for all the bat-detecting citizen scientists, right?" *I asked.*

"You got it," *said Laura.* "And what do you see?"

TK started to read off statistics. "Sixty-eight recordings of big brown bats in Northern Iowa. One hundred seventeen from Western Ohio. Ninety-three little brown bats in central Wisconsin. Forty—"

"That's right!" Laura's outburst earned her a "Shh!" from the next table. She sighed and rolled her eyes. "That's right," she repeated in an exaggerated whisper. "Tons of little brown bats have already been logged in for our region." She crossed her arms and nodded her head smartly. "So we don't need to bother with them anymore."

TK gave her a worried look. "What does that mean, don't bother with them?" he asked. "Those little guys get that white-nose syndrome Mr. Fong told us about. We have to pay attention."

"But we already *know* that," said Laura. "There is no point in doing something that's been done almost a hundred times before. We should be focused on original work. Significant discoveries." She scrolled until she found the entry for eastern red bats. Under the column for central Wisconsin, the box contained the number two. "See? If we record these bats, we'll be contributing something important. From now on, let's put all our effort into finding eastern red bats to record."

TK rubbed the top of his head. "That seems wrong, but I'm not sure why."

I finally got my tongue to work. "I know why it's wrong. It messes with the scientific method. We're supposed to be recording whatever we find, not searching only for a particular species to record. The whole point of that database is to have statistics on how common the different types of bats are in each region. If we ignore the bats we see all the time, and only record the rare ones, that's . . . that's . . ."

"It's not neutral," TK said, coming up with the perfect word. "Scientists are supposed to be neutral and just report their findings."

Laura glowered at him, then turned her monster face on me. "I can't believe you both feel this way. Don't you want to excel? Don't you guys have any ambition? How are we ever going to get to Nationals if our project is so ordinary and boring? Let's be honest, this bat detection thing is kind of lame." She slid off the stool, grabbed her kitty cat backpack, and walked right out of the library.

I'm not sure where Laura's outburst came from. She always used to be so chill. TK thinks she was just jumpy from too much iced coffee and will calm down and act like a team player soon. I'm not so sure.

YES ☐   NO ☐

Should Laura Ng Still Be My Friend?

I've been thinking a lot about Laura since she walked out on us at the library. She's changing. Or am I changing?

Even though she has lots of good qualities, she's never been the easiest person to get along with. If I were a bat, Laura would be my feeding buddy. She's really smart, so she would know right where to go to find the fattest, juiciest insects. But make no mistake—once we got there, she would dive in with her jaw open and let me fend for myself.

Maybe that's the good thing about friends: they help you but also make you do stuff for yourself. It can seem frustrating sometimes, but you end up learning more that way.

At least that's what I'm telling myself. Laura is the whole reason I'm in Science Squad to begin with. I would never have joined by myself. Science Squad seemed perfect for both of us. I like nature, I like using my brain, and I need practice (might as well be honest) doing projects with other kids. To tell you the truth, I'm not sure why Laura joined.

Laura isn't always fair. Like during that mess outside the library, when TK and I dressed up like a moth and a bat—Laura got to wear shorts and a T-shirt. It's not like we held a vote. "Here's what we're doing," she said. No discussion, just *boom.* Look how it turned out! And that ridiculous stuff she said about recording only certain kinds of bats. Then she had the nerve to walk out in a huff. You'd think she was trying to ruin our friendship on purpose.

Maybe I'm just imagining things. I hope so.

I Asked That Question Again

Imagine the world is a piece of glass, and you're going along your merry way, and then you notice a crack. Just a little one. But while you're squatting down, trying to patch up the crack, you hear this popping sound behind you.

It's another crack. A bigger one. You run over there, but the crack keeps getting longer, like a cartoon artist is scratching her pen over a piece of paper. You can't even run fast enough to keep up with the end of the jagged line. And then a bunch of little cracks grow out of the big one, the same way streams and tributaries grow off a river.

Well anyway, that's how my life is feeling right now. First all the fundraising flops, and then the thing with Laura, and now a thing with Mom.

It's my fault. I asked the Forbidden Question again. I know I shouldn't have, but it just seems like I'm always waiting for something, and I just wanted something to happen now. It was getting me down.

80

It all started when I went for a bike ride with TK. We talked about how much we can't wait to get to high school, how he can't wait to learn to drive, how I can't wait for Mom and Ginger to get married. After that, I thought for one crazy second that maybe I could speed up one of those things and push it along.

As soon as Mom got home from work, I took the plunge. With Ginger sitting right there, and Mom still hanging up her keys and taking off her purse, I said, "So, when are you guys getting married?"

Ginger's eyes got wide, but she clamped her mouth shut. Mom's eyes were wide too, but she had plenty to say. "When? When we're ready. When it's the right time. Who's getting married here? You or me? This is a huge decision, and having you poking at me about it all the time is not making it any easier. The wrong decision could ruin a lot of lives, in case you hadn't noticed."

That's when Ginger stood up, smacked her chair against the table, and marched off to her composing lair, slamming the door behind her.

I couldn't take it. I was already crying when I shouted at Mom, "Nice going. Now I'll never have two parents."

I ran up here to my room. I tried to calm down by reading a bat research website. Boy, was that the wrong thing to do.

As if all these problems with the humans in my life weren't enough, guess what I just read? Bat detectors in Wisconsin are recording fewer and fewer of the little brown bat sounds. Scientists think that means the species is being killed off by that awful bat disease, white-nose syndrome.

And if that weren't depressing enough, I found out something worse. Sometimes WNS is spread by people who actually love bats! It's an accident, but still, it's happening. Spelunkers in wild caves and tourists in show caves bring it in on their clothes. All you have to do is wear the same sneakers or jacket in an infected cave, and then again someplace else, and you can spread a few spores of the fungus. And boom, you've killed a bunch of bats. Without even knowing it, you've done something awful.

I think I'll text TK. No, wait. His mom was taking him to a movie tonight. So I guess I'll try my luck with Laura. For all her faults, she's a pretty good listener. Or at least she used to be.

My Life Continues
to Fall Apart

Laura didn't answer my text last night. This morning I finally heard from her. I'll copy it from my phone.

Me: Hi, world is falling apart, but otherwise I'm good You?

L: Hi. Sorry ur having a bad day

Me: More like a bad life LOL

It's the whole Mom/ginger thing

L: Yeah so

Me: Yeah? So?

L: you should come over to talk

Me: you are so sweet

Be right there

It sounded like Laura might be back to her old self. Wishful thinking, I guess. Mom was at work and Ginger's lair door was closed, so I left a note. "Went to Laura's." Usually I'd draw a heart, but I just didn't have it in me.

By the time I pedaled up Laura's driveway, I was already feeling better. They said in health class last year that exercise helps your emotional state, but I think it was relief that I was going to talk to someone who really understood me.

That's how innocent I was, considering what actually happened. But I don't want to jump ahead.

Anyway, Laura's dad was doing something to their lawn, like he always is.

"Nice and green today, Mr. Ng," I called, feeling almost cheery.

"Hello, Bru." I have trouble reading Mr. Ng. He's usually a pretty serious guy. But today he appeared especially intense. Maybe he was trying to warn me about Laura's mood. Unfortunately, I didn't pick up on the message.

Laura was in her room, sitting on her bed. Leotards and tights and different types of dance shoes lay scattered all over her quilt. The clothes were crumpled and draped haphazardly, like she'd picked up each item, given it a squeeze, and tossed it nearby. It looked like a dress rehearsal gone wrong.

Then I saw the stress lines around her mouth and the crease in her forehead. "What's going on?" I asked, cautiously moving a pair of sparkly purple tights so I could sit down. If I'm being completely honest, I was kind of disappointed not to start talking about my own issues right away. But this looked like an emergency. "What's with all the dance stuff?"

Her answer caught me off guard. "The bat project," she said. "Science Squad." I waited, but she just pulled her knees up to her chin and sighed.

"What about Science Squad?"

When she finally met my gaze, her eyes looked darker brown than usual. "I just want to dance. I'm not dancing enough." She grabbed a scuffed-up white ballet slipper and pressed it to her stomach. "That's what I really want to do."

I wasn't quite understanding where she was going with it. "So, dance more," I said, trying to be super helpful.

"No, it's not that easy. I need more time and energy for dancing, Bru. I'm sorry." Her head bowed forward, and she mumbled to her feet, "I'm quitting Science Squad. It's just not for me."

It was like an alien had zapped me with a ray that froze my whole nervous system. So many thoughts cycloned around my head, like bats at the mouth of a cave. *But we joined Science Squad together. Why can't you do both things? Why is everybody letting me down?* But nothing would come out of my mouth.

My legs shook when I stood up. My eyes refused to turn toward her. I think I said something brilliant like, "Fine, whatever." And I walked to the bedroom door. I do remember what I said next: "Have a nice life."

So, I guess I'm down one friend. Who needs a traitor, anyway? The bats are better off without her, and so am I.

Maybe I should have said something. No. There was nothing I could say that wouldn't sound like begging. And her mind was obviously made up.

But you know what? Brubeck Farrell can definitely get her feelings hurt. Now I'm starting to feel sad.

TK wants to bike out to the reservoir for a picnic lunch. Something about "communing with the bats in their natural habitat," whatever that means. I mean, the sun is out and they're asleep. Oh, well. Maybe the exercise will help.

Or maybe I'll feel sad for the rest of my life.

A Reservoir Full of Tears

It should have been an okay but not super exciting way to spend a hot afternoon. The comfort level was not too impressive: 95 degree heat, 98 percent humidity, and we were sitting on rocks at the edge of the water reservoir just outside of town.

TK, wiping copious amounts of sweat off his face with the sleeve of his T-shirt, got all teachery:

"We can watch all the best bat videos in the world," he said, "but it's not the same as seeing them for real, outside, flying around. Or experiencing their environment, as we are right now." He gestured at the big, perfectly round pond full of brown water. "So, any guesses why I chose the reservoir?"

"Because you wanted to torture me with the world's longest, hottest bike ride?" I suggested.

"Two reasons." TK sounded much too perky as he untied the small cooler from the back of his bike. "Hint: the first one has to do with bats."

I looked at my toes wiggling in my sandals and pushed out a sigh from way down by my tailbone. My brain was a big ball of mush. I wished Laura were there. She'd have fifteen different answers. Plus, she'd be there, smiling at me, which would just make everything better.

Thinking about Laura made my stomach ache, way up by my heart.

"I have no idea why we're here," I admitted. A lump in my throat made the words hard to get out.

TK handed me a sandwich wrapped in parchment paper. Then he held out his metal water bottle and wiggled it back and forth. "Here's another hint."

"The bats are thirsty?" I was getting sick of the game. A mosquito bit my thigh, and I smacked it with a vengeance.

"Yes! There you go."

"You're glad I got bitten?" I slammed my sandwich down. "What is your *deal?*"

"What's *my* deal?" TK cocked his head. "You're the one with the deal. I thought you loved talking about bats. And why did you tell me not to invite Laura?"

I waved my hands around like insects were attacking me, but I just wanted him to stop talking about Laura. "She quit Science Squad, okay? And I'm just kind of annoyed."

"She quit? Why?"

"Never mind. Forget it. Forget her. Tell me about the bats and the reservoir." My eyes were full of tears and my cheeks were hot. I just wanted to go home.

TK spoke quietly. "Insects love water. And lots of bats eat insects, so they come to where the bugs are. That's why we're at the water. Sort of a tribute to the bats."

It made sense, and on any other day I would have thought it was a great idea. All I could do was nod and poke at my sandwich without looking up.

Still trying to get the old Bru back, TK continued. "Knowing where to get food is important before you decide where you're going to live, right? Say, for example, that two people wanted to get married and start a life together. They would decide where to buy a house based on what was available in the neighborhood—grocery stores, good schools if they wanted kids, a place to worship, etc. Animals do that too. They want to feel like they and their babies will be as safe and well fed as possible . . . blah blah blah."

He didn't actually say blah blah blah, but I stopped listening and floated away in my head. All that talk of cozy human homes made me think of Mom and Ginger and how much I wanted us to be a real, official family. I thought about it so hard that I started to cry. Right there by the stupid reservoir, sitting on a rock and holding a sandwich, I totally lost it.

A warm hand pressed on my shoulder. Good old TK, always ready with a hug. I sobbed so hard I probably scared away all the insects. My tears could have made the reservoir overflow.

Once I'd calmed down a little, TK said, "You and Laura—you're not friends anymore?" The best I could do was make a sound like an animal caught in a trap. With my head on his shoulder, he whispered right into my ear. "I get the feeling there's something even bigger that's making you sad."

It all poured out, like bats flying out of the mine at sundown. How much I want Mom and Ginger to get married, how furious I am with Laura for quitting Science Squad, how exasperated I am that we can't get decent equipment for our bat project. Interesting that the bat thing was last on the list, considering how important it's seemed recently.

Anyway, he listened without talking. Then, instead of giving me a bunch of know-it-all grown-up advice, he just said, "Bru, you have the biggest brain and heart of anyone I know. Things are going to work out. I just know it."

I hugged him back and told him what a terrific friend he is. Now I just wish I believed him that things would be okay.

Ginger was home when I got back from the reservoir. I guess I was dragging because she put one hand on my shoulder and brushed back my bangs with the other hand. "Everything good, Jazz?"

Something about that nickname she uses when she's being extra nice choked me up. I thought about how much I want her to be my other official mom, and that got me even more choked up. The last thing I felt like doing was talking about my problems all over again. So I pulled away—I couldn't even look her in the eye because I was trying not to sob—and I said, "I have Science Squad stuff to do."

And I ran up to my room. I probably hurt her feelings, which is the exact opposite of what I wanted. Just like I really want to help the bats, but being stuck with lousy equipment makes it impossible to help. Why doesn't stuff ever work out the way it's supposed to?

Now I'm lying on my bed and watching a spider crawl super slowly across my ceiling, wandering back and forth like it doesn't know where it's going or what it's trying to do. I can relate.

A minute ago, I heard Mom drive up and come in the house. She's been out at her painting class or yoga or something. Now the music is starting, like it always does as soon as she comes inside. Old jazz, her favorite. I recognize the high-flying, crazy trumpet sound of Dizzy Gillespie, who had the biggest, puffiest cheeks of any person in history.

And I'm thinking about Dave Brubeck, the jazz piano player Mom named me after. She told me a bunch of times that she named me that because the only thing she loved more than jazz was me.

I'm pretty sure Ginger's in that category too, but Mom won't admit it. Why?

I have to wonder if there's another reason I'm connected to Dave Brubeck. His most famous song is called "Take Five" because it has five beats per bar instead of four, like a normal song would. In a way, that could describe me. A girl with an awkward number of beats.

But right now, two is my favorite number. I want to have two moms and two best friends, not one of each.

Oh, well. For now, one is better than none. TK invited me over to his uncle's tomorrow. Maybe that will cheer me up.

Fundraising
Almost-Not-a-Flop

TK has the coolest uncle. And they look so different that it's hard to believe they're related. TK is tall and skinny with a long, narrow face and high cheekbones and very dark skin. His Uncle Morris is short, round as a beach ball, mostly bald, and has much lighter skin. He's also a lot sillier than TK.

Like this afternoon, Uncle Morris (all TK's friends are supposed to call him that) was telling us about this old van with ridiculously big wheels he used to have. To show just how big the wheels were, he opened a purple umbrella and twirled it by his hip while he pranced across the living room, going "Vroom room! Beep beep!" I almost choked on my lemonade, laughing.

Actually, that story led into a surprising way to spend our afternoon: "Speaking of vans," he said, "I need to make a delivery. You kids want to come? I'll buy you a soda when we're through. Plus, Ms. Mikah is a fun lady."

95

"If there's an icy beverage at the end, count me in," said TK, pushing his blue mirrored sunglasses up his nose and flashing a toothy grin. He often helps Uncle Morris with delivery jobs. And I was intrigued to meet somebody with the cool name of Ms. Mikah. She sounded like the director of a spy school for kids.

In the back of the mud-splattered pickup truck, a mound of something was covered in a black plastic sheeting and bound with twine. TK sat in the middle of the front seat, straddling a trash can and two cupholders. After Uncle Morris tossed some fast food wrappers into a bin at the edge of the driveway, I settled in by the window.

It was like anti-stress therapy, being squashed in next to my best friend (now that Laura is apparently out of the running), speeding down the highway, with old rock songs blasting from the radio. At the edge of farm country, the sunlight through the clouds made the soybean crops glow a space-alien green. I rolled down the window with one of those old-fashioned cranks. The smell of hay and cow dung struck my nose in a way that made me truly happy for the first time in days.

Beyond the farmers' fields, the woods looked a little spooky. I thought about how much the bats must like this area, which is where the Patel twins are supposed to be detecting. For a second I considered texting them, but Uncle Morris suddenly took a sharp turn onto an unpaved driveway. "Here we are!"

A big wooden sign said "Mikah Garden Center." A woman with wide hips and the biceps of a weightlifter stood outside a greenhouse, waving at us.

"That's Carol," said Uncle Morris with a dreamy smile. "I mean Ms. Mikah."

"She looks nice." When TK said that and waggled his eyebrows at me, it was all I could do not to break out in giggles. Seems like Uncle Morris has a crush!

Ms. Mikah *was* nice. After we'd helped her and Uncle Morris unload the bags of fertilizer from the back of his truck, she made us all iced tea. We sat on her back porch, looking out over rows of summer squash, corn, and beans. Noticing the woods behind, I thought of the bats again.

"Do you ever see bats around here at night, Ms. Mikah?" I asked. Out of the corner of my eye, I saw TK slowly shake his head. But I didn't care. I'm a proud citizen scientist who wants everybody to appreciate bats. "There are probably lots in that forest."

"Oh, my, yes," she said. "In fact, look at this." When she got up and walked to the fence at the edge of her porch, I followed. "See that wooden box on a pole?"

It was like a huge birdhouse. "Is that what I think it is?" I asked.

"I made that bat house myself," she said with a gleam in her eye. "Every bat has a friend in Carol Mikah."

Finally, TK got into the act. He came up behind us. "We do this citizen science thing called Science Squad," he said. "We're studying bats."

Uncle Morris chuckled. "When I was your age, nothing would've made me study in the summertime."

"It's fun," TK protested. "Anyway, we use a bat detector to listen for bat calls."

Ms. Mikah leaned over to grab her iced tea. "How fascinating! So, you're what? Keeping track of what types of bats are in the area?"

"That's right," I said, exchanging a look with TK, who raised his thumb in encouragement. No risk, no reward, as somebody once said. I took the plunge. "We're trying to raise money to get better detection equipment. I don't suppose you'd be willing to donate to our Science Squad fund?"

TK's hands were over his mouth and his eyes were wide, like he'd just watched me bet a million bucks at a Vegas poker game.

When Ms. Mikah turned to him, his face relaxed into a charming grin. "I'd be glad to help you kids out," she said. "Hang on, I'll get my checkbook."

She hustled into her house. As the screen door closed, Uncle Morris sighed. "What a lady."

I'm not proud of what I was thinking: *She's very nice. But is she rich?*

Ms. Mikah popped back out, waving a check between thumb and forefinger. "Here you go, dears. I'll donate in the name of my business, since bats are so important to our ecology. And I would have no business at all without the ecology."

I could hardly breathe, waiting to see the amount on that check.

"Could you send me a receipt for tax purposes?"

We both nodded vigorously, even though we had no idea how to get her a receipt. We would figure it out. I moved to the edge of my iron patio seat. TK actually stretched his hand out toward the check. Rude! His mouth was half open, his tongue slightly out. He was practically drooling.

Finally, Ms. Mikah handed over the check. TK pinned it down with his thumb so the breeze wouldn't snatch it. We both leaned in to peek. Would we be able to order our new bat detector?

The check was for $50. So, that's a hard no.

I realize this was generous of her, but it's way less than the amount we need. Not looking disappointed at that number was one of the most difficult things I've ever done. TK and I deserve acting awards for how enthusiastically we said, "Thank you so much!"

Bummer. No new bat detector. Yet. But I'm not too in the dumps about it. I have another idea I'm percolating in my mind. I'm not sure if it'll work yet. It depends on how our detecting expedition goes tonight . . .

Echo Series D Meets the BatWrong −5000

We did it! We got a bat recording. It's only 23 seconds long, and it took us about seventeen tries, but we got it! Not to brag, but actually, *I* got it. Although admittedly I had an unfair advantage. While TK kept trying to get Mr. Pinter's old and broken Echo Series D to work, I whipped out the homemade heterodyne that Ginger and I had built. Apparently my soldering skills are solid.

But I have to give TK some credit. He had the excellent idea of approaching the mine from the other side, over by Decker Woods. That way, we could have a chance to record different species of bats. The ones from the mine are probably just too far away for our equipment. But everybody in Ingotville has seen bats flying out of those woods at dusk. I read that silver-haired bats are one of the most common tree bats in Wisconsin. So that's what I'm expecting. Laura would be happy to hear that we might have eastern reds here. That is, she would if I were speaking to her, which I'm not.

We also had to figure out the problem of how to record. These heterodyne detectors don't have recorders in them. Mom came up with a pretty brilliant solution while she, TK, and I were eating dinner at Fish & Chips before we went detecting. She suggested we use my phone recorder app.

At first, stupid me, I thought she meant to just hold the phone up to the bats instead of the detector. "That won't work," I said. "The sounds are ultrasonic, so we'd need a special microphone."

"Actually, we could," said TK, dipping a hunk of haddock into mustard sauce. "Turns out there are bat detector apps."

"What? And you didn't tell me?"

With his mouth full, he said, "The apps are free, but you have to buy like two hundred dollars' worth of equipment to make the apps *do* anything. Didn't think that was worth mentioning, given our situation."

"If I may continue explaining my idea?" Mom continued. "I meant that you could use your regular memo recorder on your phone to record the sound that comes out of the speakers on the detector. Because the detector has the correct kind of mic, right?"

"Right," I said. I hate it when she's right.

"That would totally work," said TK. "Thanks, Ms. Farrell!"

And it did work, at least on the machine Ginger helped me build. Mr. Pinter's is a hopeless case. At first I ended up with a bunch of two-second bursts of hissing and blips. (I notice a lot of those get posted on bat detector sites, but I think that's lame.) But then I got this one long, 23-second recording. We might just be getting the hang of this.

Tomorrow we'll try to find out what type of bat we recorded. Right now, I'm too sleepy.

TBD BAT RECORDING

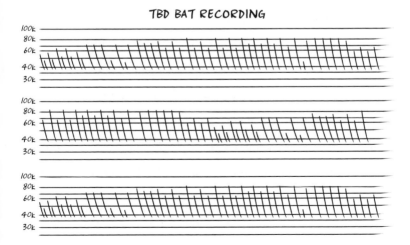

Will the Noisy Bat Please Flap Its Wing?

TK and I usually get along pretty well. But when it comes to bat call classification, apparently we turn into werewolves. We were ready to rip each other's heads off by the time he left today . . .

First we had to agree on what kind of sound we'd recorded. Since our equipment isn't very sophisticated, we were relying on my phone's recording of what came out of the BatWrong –5000. I put that file into the bat listening database, hoping it would turn it into a spectrogram. But no, we got an error message saying the sound quality was too low. Grrrrr! So we were left with just the sounds to compare, since we couldn't see a picture of the frequencies.

We both agreed it was a bat sound, not mechanical or insect sounds. Although to be perfectly honest, we couldn't stand the thought of it *not* being bats. It *had* to be bats. Then we had to figure out what type of bat it was. TK thought the pitch and the timing of the chirps matched the field guide for the echolocation calls of hoary bats. But then we found another recording of hoary bats—I guess it was made with different equipment—and it sounded totally different.

Meanwhile, I was absolutely sure we had recorded silver-haired bats, since they're common in our part of central Wisconsin. As far as I'd read, they're more common than the hoary bat, so that's more likely that was what we recorded. Plus, the hoary bat's chirps were farther apart than what we captured on our recording.

"But the recording of the silver-haired bat in the field guide makes the chirps sound closer together than what we got," TK complained.

"Yeah, but ours is more like the silver-haired one than the hoary one."

"No, it's more like my kind."

"No, my kind."

This went on for a while. I missed Laura's input. A third vote would have moved things along. Doesn't she know how much she mattered to Science Squad? Instead, TK and I were stuck with a stalemate.

Finally, he huffed and put his hands in the air. "Fine. We'll call it a silver-haired bat."

I'd won, but I felt kind of bad about being so feisty toward TK. "The experts who curate the database will make the final decision," I said, hoping that would make him feel better.

But we weren't finished. The next question was what type of call it was: searching for food, social "talking," or the sounds they make while they're feeding. We must have listened a hundred times to our recording plus a bunch of examples in the field guide, squabbling the whole time.

"This is dumb," TK finally said. "We don't have a good enough recording."

"That's the first thing we've really agreed on all day."

"We *have* to get some better equipment," TK said.

And that was the second thing we agreed on. Maybe our friendship will survive after all.

WNAR, We Need You!

This time, for once, I'm pretty sure an idea I had is as great as it seemed when it first came into my brain.

I was thinking about how we could convince people to be interested in bats and help us raise money. How we could get the community to care. The answer? Educate them! Show them the work we've done so far. Maybe it isn't all that much, but the clip of the silvered-haired bat—or hoary bat, or whatever it was—is pretty cool.

But, how to share it with lots of people? We could put it on social media, but with no video it would never go viral. I thought about printing the URL of our bat sound on postcards. But A) postcards cost money, B) postcards waste trees, and C) who's going to bother to type in a URL?

Then the answer dawned on me: *The Levin Crowne Show!*

Half the people in this town listen to Levin Crowne's news and silliness on weekday mornings. And sometimes he *plays audio clips listeners send in. We could do an ad for our Science Squad fundraiser.*

I texted TK to come over ASAP. After I told him my idea, he added an interesting twist: "Instead of some boring ad, we send the bat clip to the show. It's so strange, he's got to love it." I opened my mouth to say that the sound of some bat squeaks was not going to cut it. But TK was way ahead of me. "We can include an announcement about Science Squad, saying we're trying to raise money. And we can point out how important and awesome bats are."

"Can I give you a hug, TK?"

"Yes, Ms. Brubeck Farrell. Bring it."

After the hug, we got to work writing a script. Here's what we came up with:

> *Hey, Ingotville. Hey, Enderby. Hey, everybody who can hear this. We are kids from the Science Squad of central Wisconsin, and we are trying to save the bats. You know, the little critters you hear squeaking and chirping at night. They aren't scary or dangerous—they're actually really important! They eat*

mosquitoes and pollinate plants. To help
us save the bats, go to our FundUp page,
Bats4Wisconsin. Thanks!

I recorded the ad on my voice recorder app while TK
set up the FundUp page. He needed an adult to sign off on
it, but a quick call to his mom took care of that.

Things didn't go as well for me. It took me five tries
to say my lines with no mistakes while sounding like the
perfect combo of cheery and responsible.

"You nailed it," TK assured me when he heard my fifth
recording. "Want to text it to Laura and see what she
thinks?"

"No." The word plopped out like a stone falling into a
river.

"Why not?"

I glanced up at TK and shrugged. His pursed lips and
scrunched-up eyebrows screamed that he was dying to ask
more but could tell I didn't want to talk about it. TK knows
when to leave things alone. He just said, "Okay, then. Now
what?"

I pulled him into the hallway and pointed to the closed
door of Ginger's composing lair. "Now I face the beast to

complete the quest." Giving him another quick hug, I said, "Wish me luck. I'll text you later." I let him show himself out (it's not like he didn't know the way).

When I tapped lightly on Ginger's door, she grunted, "Come in." It was tempting to make a joke about how much she sounded like a Kodiak bear. But her puffy eyes, hunched shoulders, and tense jaw—not to mention the empty coffee pot—warned me that she might pull a real Kodiak move and rip off my head.

"Hey, Ginger, how's it going?"

"It's not going. Anywhere." Her voice sounded like someone had their hands around her throat.

"Listen, I was just wondering if you could help me with something super quick." I held my breath.

She sucked in air through her teeth, closed her eyes, and let the air out slowly, like she was finding her center. Then she actually managed a small smile. "Sure, Jazz. What's up?"

It only took her a few minutes to show me how to put the bat sound file and my voice file on a program called Thundersound. Next she layered the files together so they played at the same time. Then she helped me edit the clip so it was exactly twenty seconds, which is the time limit for submissions to *The Levin Crowne Show.*

Honestly, I think helping me relaxed her. By the time we were done, we were laughing and joking around. Ginger and I are great together. Wish my Mom could see that . . .

Anyway, I just submitted the file on the WNAR–102.5 website. Come on, Mr. Crowne, do the right thing!

The Difference between Tree Bats and Cave Bats

Some bats live in caves or mines. This gives them a safe, protected place to hibernate over the winter. Cave bats might also roost in barns and attics.

Tree bats migrate south for the winter. They live in holes in tree trunks or under loose bark. A single region can be home to both cave bats and tree bats. Human-made bat boxes can give bats a safe place to roost in areas where there aren't enough natural habitats.

The End of the World

Last night TK and I texted while we both looked online for neat bat facts. Here's what I found: Indiana bats, which are an endangered species, look very similar to some other types, like little brown bats. But the Indianas have pink lips and bigger feet!

And here's a factoid TK found: lots of people don't want bats living in their barns or attics, but they also don't want to hurt the bats. So "humane bat removal" is now a thing. You do it by sealing up every single crack and crevice except one, and then you put a little one-way door on that last opening so the bats can go out but not back in.

Truth: I'm writing about bats right now because if I write about what's actually on my mind, I'll start crying.

But if I don't write about it, that's even worse. So here goes:

Last night everything seemed like it was going to be okay. *Seemed* like. Past tense. This morning everything changed. And speaking of tense, this morning is probably the most tense I've ever been in my whole life.

I'd just had breakfast with Mom and Ginger. We had planned a fun Sunday, maybe driving down to Lake Wilbur for a picnic. Instead, my whole life exploded. And it's all my fault.

I was trying to pick which shorts to wear. Mom and Ginger were in the kitchen, talking about lunch. Or so I thought. But the vibe in the house turned weird. I couldn't hear what they were saying, but I could tell their voices were stressed. I came out of my room and sat on the landing, just out of sight.

I almost wish I hadn't eavesdropped. Now all I can think is the worst possible thing. It was a very quiet fight, almost whispered. But it was a fight for the ages. Here's what I could hear:

Mom: Is it that important to you? (This is when I started listening. It seems like they'd been talking about marriage before I came out of my room.)

Ginger: Well, let's just say it would show trust in me. And respect. After all this time together.

Mom: You don't think I respect you?

114

Ginger: I'm not saying that. But haven't I earned the right to . . .

Mom: Earned? I didn't know you had a job here, and I had to pay you.

Ginger: That's not what I mean, and you know it. I just feel like maybe it's time we were more permanent. Time that you really committed to this relationship.

Mom: Oh, nice. So now I'm not committed to you? After five years you say that? Have I done anything, any single thing, to make you think I'm not committed to you?

Ginger: My point is, you have a hang-up about this.

Mom: No, I have a hang-up about jumping into a lifelong decision before I'm absolutely sure . . .

Ginger: What's it going to take to make you absolutely sure? What else can I possibly do?

Mom: Did Brubeck put you up to this? Does she often talk to you about this?

Ginger: No. It's just that she brought it up yesterday, and it got me thinking. If you don't believe in us as a couple yet, till death do us part, maybe we need a break.

Next came a horrible, terrible, big, scary pause when nobody said anything. Then this:

Mom: Maybe you're right. Maybe we need a break.

I should have jumped down the stairs and said "No, Mom, she's not right." And I should never have been pushing them about marriage. This is all my fault. I have to get out of the house or I'll start screaming. I'll tell Mom I'm going to the library. I just heard Ginger slam the door and rev up her motorcycle. Will I ever even see her again?

I Remember

She can't leave. They can't split up. Why didn't I just keep my mouth shut? Who cares if they're married? What's my problem?

I was going to go to TK's to cry on his shoulder. But then I'd have to explain what was wrong, and I don't have the energy. I can't talk to anyone for a while. A month ago I could've gone over to Laura's, and she'd have sat with me without saying anything. How am I supposed to get through this without her?

Right now I'm in the library, in a corner as far away from the computer stations as possible. Maybe I won't see anyone I know. Maybe I won't have to interact. The library is open until 4:30 today, so I can hide out here in the AC until then. After that, who knows? I feel like home isn't home anymore. How am I supposed to go back there?

Ginger has been with Mom—with us—for so long, it's hard to believe she ever wasn't here. But, even though I was only seven, I remember the change in Mom when she met Ginger. Instead of going out every once in a while, Mom started going out every week. Then two or three times a week. Grandma Farrell used to babysit for me back then, which was fun (she always brought those sandwich cookies with vanilla outside and chocolate centers). But I remember being annoyed that Mom was gone so much.

And then came a really scary day: I had to meet Mom's girlfriend. This was a first. She'd never had such a serious relationship before, at least not since I was born.

It was late fall, right before Thanksgiving, when the three of us first went out for dinner. Looking back, that's probably because Mom wanted to invite Ginger for Thanksgiving but was testing things out with me first.

Mom let me choose my outfit. I went with cords and a fluffy purple sweater. Wow, I was nervous. Can I be honest? I don't think I wanted to like Ginger. I just wanted it to be Mom and me forever. I remember having a stomachache and sitting on the couch in my fluffy purple sweater, telling Mom I didn't feel like going. And that I might throw up.

Mom sat next to me. I can still remember what she said: "If you don't like Ginger, then I will stop seeing her."

She said it so simply and quietly. So much love filled her eyes. She really meant it.

And then we got to the restaurant. It was that place that closed last year, with all the different types of pasta made from different-colored veggies. Zentini, I think it was called. Ginger was already there. She wore jeans and a charcoal-gray sweatshirt, and her glasses were chunky blue frames. She had a smile like a giant stuffed animal, so friendly and welcoming. Her hair was burgundy and pink back then.

She said, "Hi, Brubeck. I'm Ginger. May I call you Bru?" When I nodded, she handed me a flat paper bag. "I hear you like to read, Bru."

In the bag was the first volume of the *Marissa Underground* series. Back then I'd never heard of it, but that night, I read the whole thing, and obviously it's the greatest graphic novel series of all time!

So, anyway, I loved Ginger right away. Thanksgiving was great. She started coming over all the time. By the end of the school year, she officially moved in. Mom gave up her "study," as she called it, for Ginger to use as a composing lair.

So Ginger can't leave. She's part of our house. It would be like ripping off the roof during a Wisconsin winter.

Looks like the library is closing, so I'd better find someplace else to go. Definitely not ready to go home.

You Never Know
Who's Listening

Sometimes I think I'd like to live in this huge concrete pipe in the dried-up creek bed. At least in summertime. The concrete is cool and shady. My breath echoes a little. So does the scratching of my pen on the paper. Interesting bugs and other creatures come to visit me.

I wandered over here today after the library closed. When I first curled up in the pipe, feeling so sad I couldn't even write in my journal, I saw the following folks:

1. A big, shiny black cricket that hopped from rock to rock.

2. Three daddy longlegs, one of which spent the whole time upside down at the top of the pipe.

3. A bumblebee, big and fat, that looked tired, so I scooped it up onto a maple leaf and set it on a dandelion.

4. A toad. I picked it up. Its little feet felt so funny on my palm when it jumped off again.

121

5. A bullfrog. It wasn't technically in the pipe, but I saw it puffing out its neck in the creek bed. I hope it has found someplace wetter to hang out.

6. Tons of mosquitoes. Actually I can feel them, not see them. Especially in the last hour.

7. A human.

I really should get home for dinner, especially since I skipped lunch. Mom just texted to ask if I was okay. I sent back a thumbs-up, which wouldn't satisfy her for long. It's almost too dark to write in my journal anyway. But I have to get down what just happened.

A few minutes ago, I was just sitting here, feeling so low, like my bones were made of lead. I heard a little tick on the concrete pipe.

"Hey, can I come in?" And Ginger's burgundy head appeared. I've hidden here a bunch of times before, and a couple years ago I told her about my secret concrete pipe. I guess she was paying attention. She knew right where to find me.

Oh, boy. I could not handle the lecture I knew she had ready for me. It was going to be "That fight with your mom wasn't as bad as it sounded," or "Every couple goes through rough patches," or "It's not your fault." The only thing she could possibly say that would make me feel better was, "Your mom and I are getting married."

At least that's what I thought. But I was wrong. The next words out of her mouth knocked me sideways and took away at least 50 percent of the gloom I was feeling.

"I listened to the bat sounds you recorded, since you left a copy in the recording-studio program on my computer." It was a weird way for Ginger to begin a pep talk about relationships. I sat up. "Bru, the bat call is just fascinating. I'm so inspired. All those squeaks and cries are so strange and otherworldly, like a race of gentle space aliens. I was wondering—would it be okay with you if I used that clip in my score for *Light Rescuer 2*?"

Ginger was standing at the pipe's entrance, leaning on both her forearms against the rim. I threw my arms around her waist. She hugged me back. "I take it that's a yes?"

"Yes, yes, yes, yes!"

"And if you make more recordings of bats, will you let me use those too?"

My laugh echoed down the pipe. "You mean *when* we make more recordings. I would be so proud to be part of your music."

Ginger took a step back and held both my hands. "Believe me, Jazz, you're always part of my music."

After hearing those beautiful words, I dared to ask the Important Question: "So, you're not leaving?"

"Leaving? I could leave you and your mom about as easily as I could leave my own skin. Now, are you coming home for dinner, or can I eat your veggie burger and sweet potato fries?"

"No way. Those fries are mine. I'll be home in half an hour."

"Make it twenty minutes."

"Deal."

I've been sitting in the concrete pipe since then, scribbling while the mosquitoes eat me alive. But it's good to write it all down while it's fresh in my mind. Maybe my life's not a total disaster. And I'll tell you something else: now I'm even more determined to get that BatSong 4000.

Two of My Favorite Things

I can't believe that whole trauma with Ginger and Mom was only yesterday. Things are almost back to normal already. Better than normal, actually.

I'm all curled up on the easy chair right now. Mom and Ginger are on the couch, watching a documentary about a jazz trumpeter named Lee Morgan. There's popcorn and sparkling water with cubes of frozen watermelon juice in it. Could there be a better summer night with my family?

But to tell the truth, I can't concentrate just now. I have to write down all the feels from earlier this evening. I'll start in the afternoon.

I was on Mom's laptop in the living room, trying to decide which I like better, Jumpster purple sneakers with silver stripes or Action8 silver sneakers with purple stars. Not that I'm getting either, since they cost over $200. But it's fun to pretend shop. Like with the BatSong 4000. It's just nice to imagine.

Anyway, I sensed someone staring at me from the entrance to the living room. It was Mom, with the weirdest look on her face. Like my ears were suddenly growing out the top of my head or something. "What?" I asked. "Is there chocolate on my face? I only had one tiny piece."

She swooped toward me, arms out. Mom has such thick brown hair. It makes me think of a waterfall, the way it flows over me when we hug. This was an extra-long hug.

"Let's go somewhere, Brubie. Just the two of us."

"Wow! You mean like Disneyland?"

She laughed. "I was thinking of something closer to home. Maybe supper and, well, what would you like to do? It's pretty nice out. We could take our dinner somewhere and eat it outside. I'll drive us to the lake, maybe."

"Do I have to do extra chores to earn this or something?"

"What? No! I just . . ." She stroked my cheek. "I just want to make sure you're okay. That we both are."

It was such a perfect idea. We decided to get fish tacos and sopaipillas at Juanita's and then figure out where to eat them. As we climbed back into the car with our food, I had one of those lightbulb moments.

"Let's go to the old mine, Mom. We can watch the bats come out to feed."

Her smile was so wide, you could have parked an eighteen-wheeler on it.

"What are you grinning at?" I asked. "I just want to show you the bats. They're cool."

Unbelievable, what she said next: "I know they're cool, Brubie. I used to watch them before you were born."

All I could do was stare for a minute. "You watched the bats? At the mine?" She nodded. "But the bats didn't move in until after the mines were abandoned."

Mom hit the steering wheel with both hands while she shrieked with laughter. "It's been forty-five years since anyone worked in those mines, sweetie. How old do you think I am?"

We both know I know she's thirty-nine years old, so I didn't bother to answer. She wiped her eyes. "Oh, thanks for that. I needed a good giggle. Let's go see the bats."

So we did. And I've got to say, it was kind of magical. Mom backed in, so we could tailgate and still see the bats come out. As they started to swarm from the crevices, I held up what was left of the last taco. "Have a nice dinner, guys," I said to them. Mom raised her iced tea to toast them too. "May you catch all the mosquitoes and come home with full tummies."

When we were done eating, we both lay back on the hood. The only light was from the moon and stars. The bats were gone, but songs of crickets, frogs, and warbling night birds filled the air with quiet music. At one point, something made a loud creaking sound up and down the scale. "That's just like a jazz solo," I said.

"Brubeck Farrell," said Mom, sitting up, "I sure did raise you right. Come on, we should get home."

So, I got two of my favorite things tonight at the same time: watching bats and spending time with Mom. Plus Juanita's fish tacos. That's three things. Plus sitting between Mom and Ginger on the couch and drinking sparkling water. That's four and five.

You know, when I think about it, I am one lucky girl.

Nocturnal Symphony

How many times have I played video games since I've known Ginger? But somehow today was the first time I really stopped to find out what she does. How important her music is to the game, I mean. When I play a game she's scored, I try to notice her music. But I had no clue how the music can make or break the experience.

Maybe it's just that she never invited me to watch her process before. And that's probably because I never asked. I've been afraid to bother her when she's in her deadline panic zone.

Today was different. I was so curious about how she planned to use the bat recording, that I actually had the nerve to knock on the door of the composing lair.

"Yeah?" Her voice sounded weak through the closed door.

It dawned on me that I should bring her something nice. "You want a fresh cup of coffee?" I called.

"That would be great, Bru."

I've been through enough of Ginger's projects to know that, the sooner her music is due, the stronger and sweeter she likes her coffee. All day long.

I poured some of the battery acid she had at the ready into the cheeriest mug I could find—mustard yellow with big red flowers on it—and stirred in three spoonfuls of sugar. Without knocking again, I pushed my way cautiously into the lair, mug first.

"Hey, you," I said gently, like I was talking to a lion that hadn't eaten in two weeks. I tried to make my smile friendly and my voice chipper. "How's it going in here? What's up with the bat sounds?"

The second I asked that question, a gleam came into her bleary eyes. "You want to see? It turned out pretty cool."

Once we'd shoved a pile of library books off the only other chair in the room, I pulled it next to hers and sat down. "So, which comes first, the music or the video?" I asked.

"Definitely the video. My job is to look at what Roger and his team of animators have done, and then add music that will intensify the emotion."

"Do you add sound effects too?" I remembered how, in the first *Light Rescuer* game, this magic sword made a shimmery sound every time my avatar picked it up. "The sound effects are amazing."

"I'll pass that along to Ted Merchant. He's the sound effects guy." She typed into her keyboard. "My job is different. Watch this. It's rough, but you'll get the idea."

Ginger has an amazing computer setup at her desk. On the right is a pretty big screen. But on the left is a super huge screen, almost as big as our TV in the living room. The fancy screens are on loan from her boss, Roger, for as long as she works for him. Nice perk!

Anyway, on the big screen an animation popped up, showing a hallway. It looked like a sketch. Not everything was colored in, and a lot of the background was plain blue.

"We are seeing the player's point of view," Ginger said. Then she typed again, and the smaller right-hand screen came to life. It showed scrolling musical staffs and a timer. The numbers ticked by so fast that I had to ask, "What is that counting?"

"Hundredths of a second."

I'm no composer, and I only read music well enough to play Bach's "Minuet in G" on the piano very slowly. But I could see notes flying past on the staff. "Shouldn't I be hearing something?"

"Later," she said. "Now pretend you're the player. Sorry, but your avatar will have to be just the letter X at this point. Those details go in later."

I grabbed the mouse and clicked on the X in a circle at the bottom of the page. The avatar started moving down the hallway.

"Enter the first door you come to on the right side of the hall."

The door was coming up. I tapped the right arrow on the keyboard, and the perspective shifted. It looked like I was entering a large room with nothing but one chair in the center.

"That's weird," I said. I looked at Ginger, wondering what to say that wouldn't hurt her feelings. "Was something else supposed to happen?"

She had a mischievous little grin on her face. "You'll see. Now, do the same thing again. But I'll turn on the music this time." She set me up so my X avatar was back in the hallway. Eerie music with long, low notes played through the speakers. I got the chills.

"Get ready to turn into that room."

My heart raced. "This music makes me afraid to open any doors."

Ginger gave me a quick squeeze with one arm. "That's a great compliment. Thank you."

There was the door again. I turned my avatar and went inside. An avalanche of shrieking violins and high-pitched pops and squeaks seemed to attack me out of nowhere. That chair in the middle of the floor was suddenly the scariest thing I'd ever seen.

The video froze, and the music cut off. Ginger started cackling. "It really works, doesn't it?"

Trying not to hyperventilate, I asked, "What just happened?"

"That was all the same video footage, but this time with my 'Hallway' music and the music for the 'Empty Chair Room.' I write different music for each room and setting." Her face glowed as she talked about her masterpiece. "For the 'Empty Chair Room,' I combined a few seconds of your bat recording with some violin and oboe digital samples. Powerful, huh?"

"Amazing." But something bothered me. "Are you just using bat sounds to scare people? That kind of defeats the purpose of my Science Squad project."

Ginger shook her head. "Not at all. Watch this. I think you'll like it." She typed, and the scene changed into a courtyard in front of a castle. The music was pleasant and flutey. "Go into those lavender doors."

I guided my X to follow her instructions. The double doors flew open when I approached. As the image shifted, I entered a room crowded with plush furniture. The music changed too. An orchestra was playing rich sounds, like in an old romantic movie. Spikey squeaks and clicks jumped out of the smoother sounds. It made me feel happy and excited, like I could expect something great and magical to happen. "Are those the bats again?"

"Yes," said Ginger. "That room is called the Sorceress' Chamber. And guess what that character keeps as pets? Bats! Big, fuzzy ones! That's a coincidence, but I couldn't resist making the connection that only you and I will know."

"That's awesome."

"Your bat sounds are awesome. I peppered them all over the score." Ginger changed the smaller screen to the title page of her score and pointed. "See? I call it my Nocturnal Symphony."

Roger Who?

No way. Totally blindsided by new information from Ginger.

I found her in the backyard, doing full-on relaxation. Lying on the chaise lounge in shorts and a bikini top, a big floppy hat over her eyes, lemonade with ice in one hand and a mystery novel in the other.

Was this the same high-strung, exhausted composer who's been skulking through the house like a zombie for the past month?

I couldn't stop myself from teasing her. I snuck up behind her chair with the sprinkler hose and gave her a chilly shower. She squealed and giggled and spritzed me with lemonade. Once she'd settled back into her comfy position, I took a seat on the grass next to her.

"Glad the job is finished, huh?" I said like Captain Obvious.

"Oh, yes."

"Did your boss like it?"

She raised the brim of her head slightly. "I sent it to him, but he hasn't responded yet. That's why I'm facing my chair in this direction." She pointed up into the hills behind our house. "So I could try to catch his vibe."

"Is there psychic energy coming off the hills or something?" Ginger is very into ancient Earth energy. It's the whole reason she moved to central Wisconsin in the first place. But her answer surprised me.

"No, not the hills. The house. I'm trying to see—I don't know—if he opens his shades maybe." She laughed. "I can't really see his shades from here. It's more of a superstitious thing."

"What are you talking about? Whose house?"

"Roger's."

I rose up on my knees and squinted at the hills. "Your boss, Roger, lives out there?"

"Yeah. Moved in about a year ago. But he spends most of his time in LA."

"I've only ever seen one house up there."

"That's the one," said Ginger. "Your mom calls it the McMansion or something."

Now I was on my feet. "Phony McMansion? Your boss lives in Phony McMansion?" I pictured the mailbox Laura and I had seen outside the gate. "R. Chen," said the label. "Your boss, Roger, is Roger Chen?"

"That's him," said Ginger. What a shame Laura wasn't there to hear that. She'd have been halfway up the hill already. Ginger continued. "He grew up in Madison, and he probably still has a house there too. He is loaded." She gazed longingly at the glint of white building among the treetops. "And he has the power to give me tons of work for years to come. Or to never use my music again." She squeezed my hand, then lay back and pulled her hat down over her face. "Sure hope he likes bats."

Jeez, so do I.

Return to Phony McMansion

Ginger has been summoned by Roger Chen, world-famous video game developer. That was her word for it—"summoned." And somehow she convinced me to come with her to the meeting this morning. She said stuff about how I could "explain my vision." I had no clue what that meant.

Mostly, I was worried she might A) drive recklessly because of stress or B) try to scratch his eyes out if he insulted her music. I was thinking maybe I could prevent a disaster. Ha ha. Imagine me being the competent, together person. That is scary.

She let off steam in the car on the way up the hill to Phony McMansion. I mean Mr. Chen's house. I should only say nice things about Mr. Chen and his house, now that I know he helps pay for our groceries. Although Ginger doesn't always talk nicely about him. Even wending up the narrow road, she was all tense about the meeting, like she didn't trust him. And she would not stop talking:

"He is a very critical guy. I mean, I know he has to be judgmental, or else he wouldn't turn out such great products, and he wouldn't be so successful. It's just that sometimes, I wonder if I have what it takes to be involved in his projects. Not that I don't think I'm a decent composer. I am. But the standards are so high. I try to challenge myself to do something that's totally new each time, and—"

"Hey! Take it easy." I put my left hand on top of her right as she brought the car to a rolling stop in front of the mansion's big iron gate.

Even through the closed windows, I could hear the dogs barking. Maybe we'd get eaten and this whole nightmare would be over quickly. But I couldn't count on that. So I went ahead with my off-the-cuff pep talk.

"You are awesome, Ginger Ogola. You are a great composer. And Mr. Chen thinks so too, or he wouldn't have hired you to write, what, four different games for him?" She nodded without looking at me. "Just trust in your awesomeness," I said.

Then a security guard showed up, restraining two Doberman pinschers on leashes. With the other hand he unlocked and opened the gate. He waved us in.

Ginger kept the car in neutral and her eyes on her lap.

"You got this," I said, trying to sound like Mom at her prime Mom moments. "You sent him the music already. If he asked you to come over, he must want to talk about it. It's not like you got called to the principal's office."

A tiny grin played over her face, so I kept at it. "He just wants to talk about the project. Not like your boss. Like a . . . like a . . ." I couldn't come up with the word I wanted.

Ginger turned to me and put the car in drive. "Like a colleague."

"Yeah. Like a colleague."

"I love you, Jazz. You're a really amazing person."

I didn't say another word all the way up to the house because I was busy wiping the tears of joy from my eyes.

And what a house! Laura would have loved it. I pretended she was standing with me, like my imaginary friend, Tina, who followed me everywhere until I was five. The entryway just inside the front door was the size of our dine-in kitchen. Mr. Chen greeted us there. He was short, with uneven patches of gray in his black hair. There was a stain—maybe mustard?—on his orange polo shirt. His jeans were a little too long for him. A guy with more important things on his mind than what he looked like. I was a fan right away.

"You must be Brubeck," he said.

"Everyone calls me Bru."

"Well, Bru, Ginger told me you made a major contribution to the absolutely amazing music our Mozart here has created for *Light Rescuer 2.* Very glad you could join us today."

I felt heat in my cheeks and hoped I wasn't blushing. Neither of them seemed to notice.

"So, you like the score, Roger?" Ginger asked as we followed him into a plush living room right out of one of the Rock Hudson movies Mom watches on TCM.

"Like it?" He said. "I love it. It's such a unique sound." He gestured for us to sit down on a sofa that swallowed me like a cloud. "Now, you said it was based on bat sounds?"

"No, it includes real bat sounds," and Ginger. She beamed at me. "Bru recorded them herself."

"Really?" Mr. Chen leaned forward. The way he listened made me feel like I was queen of the Science Squad. "Tell me how you recorded them."

I explained about our bat detectors, both Mr. Pinter's and the homemade one. "With better equipment we could get even better recordings. But the silver-haired bat squeaks turned out pretty nice, I think."

"Have you done this all on your own?" Mr. Chen asked. So I told him about Science Squad and the whole idea of citizen science. "We have a mentor at our school, Mr. Fong, but basically we're doing it ourselves." As I said this, I realized how proud I was of what TK and I had managed to accomplish. And of course I got that knot in my stomach again from missing Laura. She should have been in that mansion with me, meeting the mysterious Mr. Chen.

"Well, you are to be congratulated," Mr. Chen said, distracting me from my sad thoughts. "The bat calls are fascinating. It sort of sounds like they're saying something," Mr. Chen said. "Why do they make those sounds?"

I got to tell him about echolocation and communicating and all that. Then a nice lady in a gray dress brought us iced tea. The glasses were so big that I needed two hands to lift mine off the white marble cocktail table. He asked lots of questions about bats. Then he turned to Ginger. "Well, the bat sounds are a terrific addition to this game. And I want more."

Ginger's face froze for a second, then she said, "More? But I've already finished—"

"Oh, I mean on other games. I have three more *Light Rescuer* versions lined up, and I want bat sounds in all of them."

"Um, right," said Ginger, her voice a little too loud. "But we only have the one short clip."

"Then Bru will have to get you more, won't you, Bru?" He leaned toward me. "All those different types of bats you told me about, do they all sound different?"

145

"Yeah, that's the idea," I said, worried where this was heading.

"Then I'm counting on you to make lots of recordings to share with Ginger. Sound good?"

"Um, sure." What was I supposed to say?

After he walked us to the door, he shook Ginger's hand and said, "First-rate work. Really great."

Back in the car, I tried to explain to Ginger that I couldn't control the types of bats I recorded. She didn't seem to be listening. The smile never left her face all the way home.

Somehow TK and I will get more bat sounds.

Blue Dress

September 1! Did you hear me, universe? The first day of the ninth month is my new favorite day of the year, because the best thing I can think of will happen on that day, and I'll get to celebrate it every year after. Check this out:

I was at the county pool. Got home twenty minutes later than I'd promised, but Mom didn't seem to mind. Even though that meant she'd had to chop the salad veggies and put the lentil casserole in the oven, both of which were my responsibility. I came into the house all sheepish, ready to apologize for being late, but she just gave me a big hug as I walked in the door and said, "I love you, Brubeck. Dinner in half an hour."

And that was it. No lecture on how cell phones also double as clocks. No pile of unchopped veggies with a big sign on them saying, "We're waiting for Bru."

I should have known something was up, but I was so relieved Mom wasn't mad that I just ran to my room to change clothes. Then guilt crept into my stomach. I was about to go downstairs and offer to help Mom with dinner after all. My hand was on my bedroom doorknob when a little tap-tapping made me jump back.

Mom opened my door. Her eyes were red, and her lips were pushed together like she was trying not to cry. But she didn't exactly look sad or worried. Just distracted and jumpy.

"What's wrong?" I asked.

All she said was, "Nothing. Get dressed, sweetie."

This was an extra wacky thing to say, considering I was already wearing a T-shirt and shorts. I decided she must be joking, so I said, "You want me to put on shoes for dinner?"

She didn't laugh. "Yes, maybe your white sandals. They go with your blue dress, don't you think?"

My blue dress?! Now I was getting freaked out. Not that I don't love that dress. It's kind of a heather navy, with sleeves that reach to the elbow and have intricate beaded gray bands at their ends. And there are matching beads around the waist, V-neck, and the bottom of the skirt. Ginger says I look like the Greek goddess Diana when I wear it. Excellent dress.

What worried me was how I got that dress: at the end of May, Mom took me shopping to get clothes for Grandpa Farrell's funeral. So it was kind of creepy to hear Mom say, "The blue dress would be perfect."

I panicked just a little. "Is Ginger okay, Mommy?" I don't ever call her that anymore, but this felt like an emergency. "Did something happen to Ginger?"

"No, Brubie. Ginger's fine. We've decided to go out for dinner, that's all. We'll have the lentil casserole tomorrow." She stared at me for a second and gave me this nervous smile with her eyes a little too wide. "I guess you're surprised, right?" she asked.

"Um, yeah. Definitely surprised."

Mom and I barely said a word to each other on the way to meet Ginger at the restaurant. And I mean restaurant! Ginger had made us reservations at Dewey's, which is where people have graduation parties and anniversary dinners and fancy things like that. I figured since we were meeting Ginger there, that we were celebrating Roger's promise to give her more games to compose for. Or maybe she got some other amazing job. But even for that, Dewey's seemed over the top.

I tried to get Mom to spill the beans in the car on the way there. "So, is Ginger going to be writing TV commercials?"

She didn't answer my question. She didn't say anything. While she drove, her eyes darted around in jerky little glances, like she expected squirrels to jump out in front of the car.

My sense of dread came back, and I looked down at my fancy dress again. "Mom, what's going on?" We were at a stoplight, and Mom finally turned to look at me. Eye to eye, like she would look at an adult. I have to admit, it made my heart proud even though it scared me. "Everything's fine, Brubeck. I promise you that. Everything is fine."

Dewey's has jade-green wallpaper with sketches of scallop shells covering it. I know it sounds tacky, but it's actually kind of calming. I needed calming. I'm not used to being dressed up. It always makes me feel like everyone is staring at me and waiting for me to behave in the wrong way.

The guy who greeted us when we came in had a pleasant face, and that helped. But the background of fancy-restaurant noises jangled my nerves: silver forks on china plates, crystal glasses clinking together in toasts, the murmur of people speaking at a polite volume.

The host guy led us into a big room with lots of tables. It was mostly empty. There were only about three couples eating. And over by a set of heavy silver drapes was Ginger. I'm not sure I've ever been so glad to see her. In spite of where we were, I ran between the tables to go give her a hug.

Then I glanced back at Mom to see if she was annoyed at me for running. But she was inches behind me, and she got herself a hug from Ginger too. When the waiter came over, Mom let me get a soda, which I'm usually not allowed to have with dinner, since it's made with sugar. I wasn't scared anymore, though, since Mom and Ginger both seemed so happy.

When the waiter brought the drinks, Ginger gave him her nicest smile and said, "Thanks, Mike." It's just like Ginger to actually remember a waiter's name. "Could we please have a few minutes to talk in private before you come back for the rest of our order?"

I was a little nervous as I watched Mike walk out of the room. I knew something big was coming. I was not wrong.

"Should I tell her, Ruthie, or do you want to?" Ginger asked Mom. Mom put her hands on the table, and Ginger laid her on hand on top of it, and she gave an encouraging nod. Then Mom put her other hand on the table next to my plate. It seemed like the right thing to do, so I held her fingers too. The connection from Ginger to Mom to me was like an electrical wire. I swear my hair was standing on end. And then she said it.

"Brubeck, sweetie? Ginger and I have decided to get married."

We probably ate dinner, but I don't remember. I just remember that moment when we all held hands and Mom told me the best news I've ever heard. The wedding day is September 1.

I picked up my phone to text Laura as soon as we got back in the car. September 1 is only a month and a half away! But I put the phone back down without texting. It really stinks, not being able to tell her important stuff.

Big Mystery

I made plans to meet Jen at the pool this afternoon.
We haven't hung out since elementary school, but I figured
I needed to try and branch out now that Laura was out of
the picture.

So after having lunch at TK's, I biked home to get
my swimsuit. Now that Ginger—my almost-official-second-
mom!—is done with *Light Rescuer 2,* and since Mr. Chen isn't
ready for her to start on *LR3,* she gets out of the house
as much as possible. Must be weird, going back and forth
between having nothing to do and working 24-7. Ginger's
motorcycle was gone, and Mom was at work, of course.
What did surprise me was a red rectangle, like an envelope
or a flier stuck into the front screen door. I usually go
in the side door since the driveway is next to it, but that
red envelope caught my eye. I had to peek. It didn't look
like a store ad or restaurant menu. Nothing printed on the
outside. I pulled the screen door open so I could grab it.

It was a greeting card. For a second I assumed it was from one of Mom's clients, maybe a thank-you card or an invitation to one of those fancy parties she calls a swah-RAY, which for some reason in French is spelled "soirée." But no. The envelope said, in black marker and perfect curly handwriting, "To Brubeck Farrell."

I ripped it open right there on the stoop.

The front of the card showed a yellow Labrador dog with a big rawhide bone in his mouth. The inside said, "You were great. Take a bow-wow!" It was signed, "Yours, Roger Chen."

Ginger's boss sent me a card? Crazy. But wait, it gets crazier.

A folded-up sheet of printer paper fell out of the card. It said:

> Dear Ms. Farrell,
>
> Thank you for visiting me last week. Our discussion about bat sounds was most enlightening. I very much admire your scientific endeavors. I have no doubt that you will continue to inspire Ginger to make the very most of her considerable musical talent.

With respect and affection,

                     – Roger Chen

P.S. I have taken the liberty of contacting your Science Squad mentor, Harold Fong, to make some arrangements which I believe you will find beneficial. Kindly contact Mr. Fong for details.

I texted TK right away. We decided I should email Mr. Fong and ask if we could come to school tomorrow to meet with him. I want this mystery solved!

Eek! It's almost 2:30. I'd better get to the pool. Jen will wonder where I am. Hope Laura isn't there. Who am I kidding? I'd give anything to go to the pool with Laura. Doesn't look like it will ever happen again, though.

Waiting, Waiting . . .

I emailed Mr. Fong last night about Mr. Chen's card. He finally got back to me this morning: "I'll be in my office today working on lesson plans. Please stop by this afternoon, and we will discuss it."

So, I not only had to wait all last night, but now I have to kill half of the day today. Ugh. And now TK can't come with me because he has to help Uncle Morris with a moving job. I almost texted Laura to come with me, but then I remembered she's a traitor to me and Science Squad.

Guess I'm on my own. I'll spend time reading. Or I could draw seating plans to run by Mom and Ginger for their wedding. No, why bother? They'll just say, "People should be able to sit wherever they want." It's going to be a long morning, but I can't think of anything else to write about now. I'll finish this after I've seen Mr. Fong.

No Way!

Wow. Wow wow wow. Maybe I'll just write that word over and over. Here's a few more. Wow wow wow-wee wow.

Guess what! I went to see Mr. Fong. La dee da, no big deal.

AAAAAAAGH!

Calm down, Bru, and write what happened.

Taking a huge breath to center myself.

Wish I knew how to meditate. Ha ha.

Okay, here we go:

I showed up at school at 1:30, which is when Mr. Fong said he'd be done with his lunch. By that time, I'd convinced myself that Mr. Chen had given the school a hundred login passwords for *Light Rescuer.* Plus a huge crate of cool merchandise, like backpacks and T-shirts and water bottles. And I would be a hero.

This seemed like the most likely scenario, and I was pretty pumped about it. In fact, I was so excited to get my *Light Rescuer* keychain and mug, that the first thing out of my mouth when Mr. Fong opened his office door was, "Hi, where's the stuff?"

"What stuff?"

"The boxes of stuff from Mr. Chen."

He cocked his head in that way he does when he thinks a student has said something dumb but he's too nice to tell them. "Mr. Chen didn't send any boxes. Were you expecting him to?"

My jaw tightened. I felt cheated. How dare Mr. Chen not send all that imaginary gear I had totally made up in my twisted mind? I'm so embarrassed about it now, but I really did feel like he'd let us down. "So, what did he give us?" I must've sounded like such a spoiled child.

But like always, Mr. Fong was nice about it. "Let me show you." He had me sit in his fancy desk chair. It swivels and has wheels and springs, so you can lean back and get comfy. "Close your eyes, Bru, and put your hands out flat, palms up."

I did that. And prayed for a puppy or a pet turtle or something cool. Instead, the smooth, dry surface of paper tickled my palms. I opened my eyes. Even though I read what was in front of me, my brain couldn't take it in. It was like I was in a one-person spaceship that zoomed out of our atmosphere and I was looking at the world from the vacuum. It all seemed so unreal.

Finally I heard my name, muffled and then clearer. "Bru? Bru? Are you okay?"

I looked up at Mr. Fong's concerned face. I looked down at the mint green, extra-long check draped across my fingers. And I finally started to process what it said.

Holy-moly roly-poly guacamole! We can get a time expansion bat detector, headphones, a recorder—everything!!!

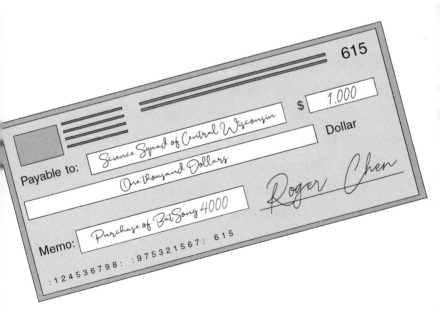

Big Mystery 2

I have a theory, but I'm not quite ready to say it. Maybe I'm afraid I'll be wrong.

TK texted that I should come to the library. Right away. Which was annoying, since I'd just gone to pick up some soy milk, onions, and tuna at Warren's Grocery. Mom likes the kind of soy milk that needs to stay refrigerated, which meant I had to bike all the way home, put the food away, then go out again to the library. Passing the grocery store again on the way, of course.

Anyway, it's super hot and muggy today, so I was not exactly Ms. Cheery when I finally dragged my sweaty self into the library. TK was at a computer and had the nerve to be impatient. "Took you long enough."

"I just . . . never mind. What's so urgent?"

He politely got off his stool so I could sit there, which cooled down my grumpiness. And the library AC started working on my body temperature. On the screen was TK's profile page on the Science Squad HQ site account.

There was a message that said, "Congratulations, Citizen Scientist! You have a new sticker." Then there was the Science Squad logo, and a sticker under it that said "Awarded for Community Education."

I studied TK's face to see if he looked like he was playing a prank. His eyes looked blank, maybe even slightly worried, and his mouth was turned down. This was no joke. "What did you do to get a sticker?" I asked.

He shrugged nervously. "I'm not sure. Didn't you get one?"

"Hang on." I hadn't been on the site all morning. I logged on in a new tab, and there it was. "Congratulations, Citizen Scientist! You have a new sticker."

I turned to TK. "Don't you have to send them proof of a project to get these?" I asked. "I didn't do that. You?"

TK shook his head. "It's a mystery."

Then I got an inkling, as Mom likes to say, just a whisper of an idea. While I was deciding whether to mention it, a new notification popped up on TK's email tab. It was from Science Squad. "We hope to see you in Chicago," read the subject line.

"No way!" TK squealed. "What is going on?"

I nudged him over and found the same email in my account. The letter was long, with lots of fine print, but the opening is all that matters. "Science Squad is pleased to invite you to represent central Wisconsin with the results of your bat detection project at our national conference in Chicago this October."

TK was losing his mind. "Nationals? We're going to Nationals? Mr. Fong must have entered our project. This is so amazing. I was hoping we'd get to go." He babbled on like that and did sort of an Irish jig around the computer stool.

Meanwhile, my mind raced. Only students can apply to present their projects at Nationals. So, it couldn't have been Mr. Fong. But we do know somebody who's been in Science Squad recently.

It's time to swallow my pride and pay Laura a visit.

The Same but Different

Outside Laura's house, I pulled my phone out of my pocket and thought about texting her. But I decided that a face-to-face interaction would tell me more about her state of mind. I didn't want her to have time to prepare.

So, instead of texting, I opened the Science Squad HQ profile page. I clicked to look at our Community Education sticker. While the sticker was still displayed on my phone, Laura's screen door opened. She leaned on the flimsy metal door and let it rock her forward and back. "Hi," she said.

"Hi."

Neither of us moved.

"What's going on?" I asked.

She stared at her bare feet and pointed at one of them. "I just found out I'm doing a solo at the dance recital coming up."

"That's nice. Congrats."

"Thanks." We fell back into silence.

After I'd moved my kickstand up and down and up and down again, I felt ridiculous. Time to get this conversation rolling. I tapped my phone screen to wake it up. The education sticker popped up in lights. Holding the screen out, I took a few paces toward Laura. "I got this today. Kind of a surprise."

She finally let go of her door and stepped out onto the stoop. When she saw the sticker, she smiled.

Was it possible we were still friends? I wanted to shout with relief. But I stayed in control. Part of me was still mad. "Do you happen to know anything about this sticker?" I asked, keeping my voice even.

Laura did a little twirl. "Maybe." Then she twirled in the other direction. "Okay, yes. I may have submitted the report that said you recorded bat sounds and put them on the radio so everyone would hear."

"So our clip made it to *The Levin Crowne Show*?! You heard it?"

"Yes. And it was a really great idea."

For half a second we looked at each other in the old way, like spirit sisters sharing the biggest secret in the world. Both of us caught ourselves at the same time and took a step back. I said, "And what about that email TK got that says we're going to Nationals?"

"That actually worked?"

"What worked?" I asked.

She laughed shyly and stepped onto the lawn. "I may have put in an application for you guys."

"I thought you quit Science Squad." My heart beat a little faster. Was she changing her mind?

But she shook her head. "I did quit. I'm out."

"So, why did you apply for Nationals?"

"To help you guys."

That answer ticked me off. "Why should you care? You quit." I felt hot tears in my eyes, but I willed them not to fall.

For the longest time, Laura stood wiggling her toes in the grass and looking at me. Then she made kind of an amazing speech. "I'm sorry if I hurt your feelings, Bru. Yours and TK's. But I'm not sorry I quit Science Squad. It just wasn't what I wanted to spend my time on. Can you understand?"

I nodded, really wanting to understand.

She continued. "And the reason I tried to get the invite to Nationals? Well, just because I don't want to do something, doesn't mean I don't want *you* to do it. Science Squad makes you and TK happy, so you should definitely keep doing it. That's what I was trying to say when I first told you I was quitting—that we can still be friends even if we don't always do the same things."

At this point my tears just went ahead and slid down my cheeks. I wanted to hug her, but I was still just a little too proud. So I put a hug into words: "Tell me when your dance recital is. Maybe TK and I can come."

Her face brightened and her whole body straightened. "That would be amazing."

"But not September 1," I added. "Mom and Ginger are getting married on September 1."

Laura's mouth fell open. Then she let out a whoop like she'd won fifty billion dollars. "Bru, that's so totally fantastic!" She whooped again, and I joined her, and before we knew it, we were hugging and hopping around on the grass like two people on the same pogo stick.

Is our friendship totally fixed? I don't know. But it's healing up nicely.

We're Going
to Need More Chairs

I can see how trying to plan a wedding could potentially break up the couple that's supposed to get married.

Fortunately, Ginger knew what to do to avoid that crisis. After ten minutes of me, Mom, her, and Laura sitting around the table talking about colors of crepe paper for decorating the backyard, she made her move. She didn't get upset. Slowly and calmly she stood, pushed in her chair, and said, "I love you all, but I can't handle this. Do whatever you want. I promise to show up and get married."

Mom was still laughing when the sound of Ginger's motorcycle had faded down the street. I need to remember that technique if I ever get married.

Laura (so awesome to be talking to her again!) had pretty much the exact opposite attitude from Ginger. She is LIVING FOR this wedding. Her energy is going to get us all through it. And the endless stream of ideas coming out of this girl. Wow! The crepe paper twists, coordinated tablecloths and paper plates, covers for the chairs. All her ideas.

I'm going to be maid of honor. Ginger's parents are coming in from Milwaukee, and Grandma Farrell will be here, obviously. Awesome news: because there isn't time, and because both my mothers are who they are, I don't have to wear some horrible floofy-poofy, flowery dress. I can wear anything. Mom says she'll buy me something new, but only if I want it. Which I do. Who passes up an offer of free clothes shopping?

Then we started talking guest list. It's not like British royalty or a rock star is getting married. Mom and Ginger only know so many people, and they both come from small families. Still, the list was at fifty people before we knew it. And a certain name on the list caught my eye. Roger Chen. Ginger wants to invite him. That's cool, but seeing his name gave me an idea.

"Mom, he has a mansion."

"He certainly does." She didn't say "Phony McMansion," but I knew she was thinking it.

"A *mansion*, Mom."

"And your point is?"

Laura got it. "O. M. G. We totally have to ask him."

"Ask him what?" Mom was still clueless, so Laura and I both said, "To have the wedding there!"

Mom's face got that look where she's forcing her cheek and forehead muscles to relax so she doesn't seem as exasperated as she feels. "I don't think that's such a great idea."

"Why not?" I pictured them saying their vows on his perfectly cut emerald-green front lawn. His dogs would sit on either side, behaving like angels. There would be champagne in long-stemmed crystal glasses. I glanced over at Laura, whose eyes were like Frisbees. She wanted this so badly. "Wouldn't it be perfect?"

Mom pointed to the chair where Ginger had been sitting before the crepe paper freaked her out. "Let's just keep it simple."

Sometimes, Mom is right. This was one of those times. Oh, well.

The three of us covered all the bases. We figured out which friends and relatives we could call to lend us stuff or bring food. Laura volunteered to design an invite on her computer. I promised to try to find a band or DJ. Mom's friend Maureen is a judge, so she'll be officiating.

At one point Laura, who's very artistic, started doodling on a piece of paper. "Whatcha got there, Ms. Laura?" I skootched over to her. She angled the paper so I could see.

Bats. She was drawing bats!

"I'll cut them out of yellow paper. Big ones and little ones. We can tape them up everywhere. And how about pins? Little bat corsages!"

Mom looked over our shoulders. "That sounds cute. And definitely cheaper than regular flower corsages." She patted Laura's shoulder. "Good work."

The mention of flowers gave me an idea. "I bet I know someone who will give us a discount on any flowers you might want." I reminded them about Carol Mikah and her gardening center. "We'll have to invite her and TK's uncle, but I bet she'd be glad to help."

"No problem," said Mom. She glanced through her notes. "All right, girls. That's everything I can think of at the moment. But we're going to need more chairs."

It's Here!

Got an email from Mr. Fong, with the subject line "It's here!" The message was exactly what I've been waiting for. The BatSong 4000 had arrived at the school.

TK's and my texts to each other practically had a head-on collision. As I stumbled through the piles of stuff we've been collecting for the wedding on my way to the door, I called out, "I'm going over to school for Science Squad!" I banged the screen door open without waiting for a reply.

Never in my life have I biked so fast. It took me 4.5 minutes to get to school. Super slowpoke TK waited for his uncle to give him a ride, so I had to pace around the building for six minutes waiting for him. I knew he'd never forgive me if I went in without him.

They don't have hall monitors during the summer, so we didn't hesitate to run to the back of the building and up the stairs to Mr. Fong's office. We both knocked frantically.

From the inside of that little room, it must've sounded like the whole neighborhood demanding to get in.

Mr. Fong chuckled at us as he opened the door, but he didn't stop us from rushing straight over to the box. He'd taken it out of the outer shipping carton, so we could see the photo of what promised to be inside. TK and I both lunged for it at once.

I was digging my thumbnail into the sealing tape on the top flap, when Mr. Fong came up behind me with a letter opener. "You know what? Why don't you let me do that, nice and neat. If we destroy the packaging, and there's something wrong with the machine, they might not take it back."

At least he was quick about it. He sliced open the tape, pulled the flap out of the box, and asked TK to hold the box while he slid out the Styrofoam protective casing. And then he sliced through more clear tape. He lifted the top half of the Styrofoam away.

And there it was. Our new best friend and research buddy, the BatSong 4000 Time Expansion Bat Detector and Recorder Bundle.

The detector didn't look that fancy. Kind of like a wide walkie-talkie. The Plektron 14.2 recorder, on the other hand, was like something off of *Star Trek*. It had these two big silver cylinders at the top, angled inward, that twisted. Mr. Fong said they were for the cables (which, after a mild panic attack, I learned were also included). Its screen looked like the machines in a hospital, and it had almost as many buttons as our TV remote control.

Things got awkward after we'd finished unpacking everything and were looking at the detector's instruction manual. Casual as anything, Mr. Fong said, "I've already talked to a bunch of science teachers about letting them borrow this."

Borrow it? I know, I know, I'm a horrible person. But that ticked me off. I mean, we did the work to get this beautiful detector. TK, me, Laura, and Ginger. Plus Mr. Chen's money. But when I complained, TK proved once again that he's a good guy through and through.

"Remember how much we wanted this detector, Bru? And how frustrated we were when we couldn't figure out how to get the money for it? Well, other people are still feeling that."

I snarled at him. Mr. Fong jumped in. "And you can multiply that feeling by every bat enthusiast, both adults and kids, in the surrounding counties." He patted the detector like it was his favorite pet. "Nobody else in our region can afford one of these."

I nodded and looked at my shoelaces, feeling guilty for being so selfish. "Fine, I'll share it. But TK and I get to use it as much as we want, right? Ginger and Mr. Chen want lots more bat recordings."

Mr. Fong laughed. "I'm sure we can come up with a schedule that's satisfactory for everyone: the well-being of the bats, the happiness of the citizen scientists, and the profit of the video gaming industry."

Obviously, TK and I are really excited to use the BatSong 4000 as soon as possible. But (and it hurts to write it) it's going to have to wait. Doing anything that doesn't involve this wedding will be impossible until September 2. Don't go away, bats. We're coming soon! Good thing it's still pretty warm in early September, so they won't be hibernating yet.

They Do!

There are still a few guests milling around. And the backyard looks like the world's most fun tornado zoomed through. I see white and purple crepe paper that broke off the folding chairs, Laura's amazing yellow tissue paper bats scattered around, paper plates everywhere, and tons of those biodegradable cups made from plant matter that Ginger made us buy. (I still don't get how they make those feel exactly like plastic.)

I am so full. And tired. And happy. I'll never be able to write down every single memory about this wedding. So I'll count down my eight favorite things. I hope I don't fall asleep before I finish this.

8. Mr. Chen showed up in a limo. And his gift to Mom and Ginger is that his limo will take them to the airport for their honeymoon trip. And he's paying for the airfare. Anywhere they want to go.

7. Speaking of which, Mom invited me on their honeymoon, but obviously she wants to have some time just

with Ginger. This is totally fine with me. I'm going to spend a week in Milwaukee, getting spoiled by my new official grandparents. I've known Leah and Jerry Ogola since I was nine, but today was the first time I ever called them Grandma and Grandpa. We all got teary, and Grandma Leah gave me such a big, smothery hug, I had to pull away just to breathe. They brought Mom and Ginger these really pretty woven floor mats they'd bought in Kenya. That's where Leah grew up.

6. One of the biggest challenges of planning this wedding so fast was finding a band to play afterward at the picnic buffet. None of the wedding bands we could afford were available. Plus, Mom doesn't like pop music.

Right up to last night, it looked like we'd end up with this rock cover band, Headroom, that plays in our area a lot. Meh. Then last night Mom's phone rang. Mom listened for a few seconds, then she just happy-screamed and pushed her fist into the air. "We got Lee Roy!"

That's Lee Roy Collins, a saxophone player she loves. She goes to lots of his shows and even helps sell his albums sometimes. As a wedding present he agreed to bring a piano player and drummer and perform for half price. So we had great jazz music, which meant a lot to Mom.

5. Carol Mikah brought flowers from her gardening center—tons of pink and yellow roses and dahlias—as her wedding present. That was so nice of her!

Of course, she carried them here in Uncle Morris's truck. Those two are really cute together. Morris did some crazy dance to one of Lee Roy's tunes that Mom said was from the 1930s. His legs flew every which way. He was limping when he left, leaning on Carol, but I think they both had a great time. Maybe there will be another wedding soon?!

4. All morning it was sprinkling on and off, but not terrible. Bummer that while my Uncle Dex and New Grandpa Jerry walked my moms (my two official moms!) down the aisle, it started to rain a little harder. But just as Mom's judge friend, Maureen, said the last part of the ceremony, about how they were now married, something amazing happened. And I'm not making this up. The rain stopped, and the sun came out. Magic.

3. I know it seems dumb to think about bats on Moms' super-special day. But hey, I'm a proud nerd and I love bats. So it was really fun to see how people reacted to Laura's tissue paper critters. Grandma Farrell called them "the cutest things," and she asked to take one home as a

party favor. One of Mom's coworkers asked me and TK a bunch of questions about the bat database. Mr. Chen said he loves the idea of yellow bats, and he might put some in a game! I hope I get a free copy to play.

2. Speaking of Laura, she hung out with me the whole day. It felt like we were back to normal. TK gave us girls some space, like he understood what we were trying to work through. But I already knew what a class act he is. It's so great to have Laura back in my life. Laura the dancer. Laura the friend, no matter what she's into.

1. I thought so hard about what to get as a wedding present. I spent hours fantasy-shopping online for fancy gifts I could never afford. And the answer was sitting right in front of me and cost $5.99.

That's how much I spent at the drugstore on a wooden frame. Then I slipped in my list of ten things I love about Ginger. Obviously, I rewrote it on a new piece of paper, so it looked nice. It's not like I'm going to rip it out of my journal. I wrapped it up pretty in yellow paper with a silver bow. When they opened it, they cried like babies and kissed me on both cheeks at once. Nailed it!

Oh my gosh, I almost forgot the very, very, very best thing about the wedding today. Mom and Ginger are married. They're actually married. Somebody pinch me.

Bat Detecting Like a Boss

I wish we had video of TK and me bat detecting last night. So much fun! Okay, not the part where I twisted my ankle and TK had to keep me from falling into a crevice on top of a mine. But otherwise: peak awesomeness.

We got there around 7:15. We were all business. Barely said a word to each other. Like real pros. It helped that this time, for once, we knew what we were doing. We'd been practicing with the BatSong 4000 detector and the Plektron 14.2 recorder for the whole week since I got home from Milwaukee. At first I was annoyed that I couldn't spend more time with my new grandparents, just because the school year was starting. But when I found out I could stay at Laura's house, I didn't mind. And it gave TK and me time to get ready for the BatSong 4000 debut.

So many bats. One set of calls sounded kind of like crickets, but really high and vibrating. We think that one is the big brown bat. Which is exciting, since the mines are full of little brown bats, a different species. TK had the idea *that maybe the big ones live in one of the barns nearby. Our research said they like to roost in buildings.*

We can't wait to go out again, but it won't be tonight. Laura's dance recital—and her solo!!!—is at 7:00 p.m. at that studio on the corner of Main and Varsity. Mom and Ginger just got back from their honeymoon, and they're driving me and TK over to see it. They went to Hawai'i. And they saw the Hawaiian hoary bat, which is native to Hawai'i! They didn't record them, though. That's my job.

What is bat detecting? Bat detecting is the collection of data about the sounds bats make when they fly around at night.

What's happening? Most bat sounds are ultrasonic—too high for the human ear—so detection requires special equipment. Citizen scientists use ultrasonic microphones to listen to and record bat sounds in their regions. They enter their findings into databases so scientists can compare and analyze the information. Each species of bat has a unique sound. They use different calls for searching for food and for communicating with other bats.

Where is it happening? Bat detection happens anywhere there are bats, which is nearly everywhere in the world. In this story, Bru would have likely worked with

the Wisconsin Bat Program (wiatri.net/
inventory/bats). The website BatDetective.
org currently has a project in Russia. And
of course, anyone can get involved in citizen
science through Zooniverse.org.

Why is it important? Collecting data
on bat sounds helps scientists learn which
types of bats live where. A decrease in the
number of a certain bat call warns that a
bat colony might be in trouble from disease
or other environmental problems. It's an
important project for citizen scientists
to help with because there's no way bat
scientists can collect data from every
forest, cave, mine, and barn.

 # In the Field

J. Paul White is a conservation biologist at the Wisconsin Department of Natural Resources. His specialty is bats, and in particular, how acoustic monitoring can be used to help the bat populations of Wisconsin. He runs a citizen-scientist acoustic monitoring program.

He is very concerned about the spread of white-nose syndrome in North America. He has called the disease "catastrophic." In 2018, he and some colleagues published a study that showed bats eat more mosquitos than previously believed, making them even more valuable friends to humans. He's also been trying to figure out how the disease moves from bat to bat by observing them in caves. "We were definitely very interested in knowing if bats might be more vulnerable to the disease based on their social behavior," he said.

Educating the public is very important to Dr. White. At the 2017 Wisconsin Bat Festival, he showed visitors how he trapped bats in nets in caves and woods so that he could study them without harming them.

Glossary

acoustic monitoring – Listening for and recording natural sounds in a particular environment.

bat call – Bats have separate calls for different purposes. Two are echolocation: 1) searching for areas where there are insects to eat, and 2) zeroing in on individual insects to eat. Bats also make sounds to communicate with other bats.

echolocation – Because they fly in the dark, bats use sound to find food and avoid bumping into things. They send out high-frequency sounds, which bounce off nearby objects and return to the bats' large ears. The closer an object is, the faster the sound returns to the bat.

heterodyne – This is the most common and least expensive type of bat detector. The user tunes the detector to a particular ultrasonic frequency. Any bat sounds in that frequency are picked up by the machine, which instantly translates those sounds into a lower frequency.

insectivore – A species of animal that survives by eating bugs. Almost all North American bat species are insectivores.

kilohertz – One thousand hertz. Abbreviated kHz. A hertz is an international unit for measuring sound frequency based on vibration cycles per second.

spectrogram – A way to "see" sound. The representation takes the form of a chart, with one axis showing time and the other showing frequency (hertz). Each sound looks unique in its spectrogram, so bat scientists can distinguish bat calls by their spectrogram images.

ultrasound – *Any sound that cannot be heard by human ears. This includes frequencies above 20 kHz. Besides bat detection, the term "ultrasound" is often used in medicine, where technicians use high-frequency sound to create images (see spectrogram) of the inside of the body based on how the sound travels (see echolocation).*

white-nose syndrome – *A fatal fungal infection destroying bat colonies in North America. The scientific name of this fungus is* Pseudogymnoascus destructans.

Selected Bibliography

Bat Conservation International, www.batcon.org.
    Accessed Sept. 5, 2018.

"Bat Detectors." Bat Conservation Trust, www.
    bats.org.uk/pages/bat_detectors.html.
    Accessed Sept. 5, 2018.

"Bat." Wildscreen Arkive, www.arkive.org/explore/
    species?q=bat. Accessed Sept. 5, 2018.

Green, Sean. "Holy Bat Sounds! Unusual Library
    Will Help Scientists Track Bat Species."
    LA Times, May 19, 2016. www.latimes.com/
    projects/bat-sounds-library. Accessed Sept. 5,
    2018.

Nuwer, Rachel. "Bats Act as Pest Control at
    Two Old Portuguese Libraries." Smithsonian.
    com, Sept. 19, 2013. www.smithsonianmag.com/
    smart-news/bats-act-as-pest-control-at-two-
    old-portuguese-libraries-9950711. Accessed
    Sept. 5, 2018.

"Why Bats?" *Bat Detective*, www.batdetective.
    org/#!/about. Accessed Sept. 5, 2018.

Zarling, Patti. "White-Nose Syndrome Sweeps
    State." *Wisconsin State Farmer*, Sept. 11,
    2017. www.wisfarmer.com/story/news/
    state/2017/09/11/white-nose-syndrome-
    sweeps-state/652557001. Accessed Sept. 5,
    2018.

About the Author

Although Anne E. Johnson has lived in New York City for a long time, she grew up in Wisconsin. She's been a fan of bats her whole life. She has written dozens of stories and books for kids, including the novels *Franni and the Duke* and *Trouble at the Scriptorium*. When she's not writing, she loves to sing Irish folk music and play her tin whistle and fiddle. Her website is AnneEJohnson.com.

About the Consultant

Chris Yahnke is a Professor of Biology at the University of Wisconsin–Stevens Point. He handled his first bat as a Peace Corps volunteer in Paraguay. He started working with the Wisconsin Bat Program in 2007 when white-nose syndrome was first detected in New York State. Since then, he and his students at UWSP have been collecting and analyzing bat acoustic calls throughout Wisconsin. He recently developed a curriculum on bats for high school students that utilizes data collected by bat detectors.

About the Illustrator

Arpad Olbey is an illustrator veteran and art director of his art studio in London. He works with paper, pencils, and paints or digital high-tech equipment, depending on the project. His wish is to combine his experience and technical knowledge to deliver the best that his creativity can give to audiences.

Welcome to the Science Squad, a citizen science organization for curious kids who love nature and science! Follow along as Squad members journal their efforts to make a difference in the world around them.

AVAILABLE NOW